The
Class

Also by Frances O'Roark Dowell

The Class

Frances O'Roark Dowell

A Caitlyn Dlouhy Book

 ATHENEUM BOOKS FOR YOUNG READERS
New York   London   Toronto   Sydney   New Delhi

ATHENEUM BOOKS FOR YOUNG READERS
An imprint of Simon & Schuster Children's Publishing Division
1230 Avenue of the Americas, New York, New York 10020

For information about special discounts for bulk purchases, please contact Simon &
Schuster Special Sales at 1-866-506-1949 or business@simonandschuster.com.
The Simon & Schuster Speakers Bureau can bring authors to your live event. For
more information or to book an event, contact the Simon & Schuster Speakers
Bureau at 1-866-248-3049 or visit our website at www.simonspeakers.com.
Also available in an Atheneum Books for Young Readers hardcover edition
Interior design by Karyn Lee
The text for this book was set in Lomba.
Manufactured in the United States of America
0820 MTN
First Atheneum Books for Young Readers paperback edition October 2020
2 4 6 8 10 9 7 5 3 1
The Library of Congress has cataloged the hardcover edition as follows:
Names: Dowell, Frances O'Roark, author.
Title: The class / Frances O'Roark Dowell.
Description: First edition. | New York : Atheneum Books for Young Readers, [2019] |
Summary: "A sixth-grade class comes together to support a classmate in need, each
of them giving their own perspective on the goings on"—Provided by publisher.
Identifiers: LCCN 2018005019 | ISBN 9781481481793 (hardcover) |
ISBN 9781481481809 (pbk) | ISBN 9781481481816 (eBook)
Subjects: | CYAC: Middle schools—Fiction. | Schools—Fiction. |
Interpersonal relations—Fiction.
Classification: LCC PZ7.D75455 Cl 2019 | DDC [Fic]—dc23
LC record available at https://lccn.loc.gov/2018005019

For Ellie Crews, Anna Maria Crescenzi,
Madeline Nielsen, and Charlotte Vollins

Chapter One

Ellie

Thursday, September 28

Ellie closed her notebook with a satisfied pat and leaned back in her seat. Done. Finished. Complete.

Hermione Granger, Fifth-Grade Muggle was ready for publication.

She'd have to figure out how to publish a book, of course. Could a sixth grader find an agent? Because Ellie was pretty sure you had to have an agent if you wanted to get a real book published, which is to say a book with a cover and pages, a book people could buy in bookstores.

Mrs. Herrera would know what to do, Ellie thought.

Mrs. Herrera was the sort of teacher who would have a dozen great ideas for getting your first novel published. Even better, she wouldn't look at Ellie like she was crazy. *Publish a book? You just started middle school and you think you can publish a book?* That was the sort of thing other adults might say, but not Mrs. Herrera.

Ellie reached into her desk and pulled out her spelling notebook. There were fifteen minutes left in study hall, plenty of time to finish her LA homework. She'd still have Spanish to do when she got home, but Spanish never took long, ten minutes tops. She could zip right through it and then get started on a new novel now that she was done with *Hermione*. It was the perfect sort of day for starting a new novel, Ellie thought as she uncapped her fountain pen, the air just cool enough that she could sit on the front porch swing wearing her cozy green sweater, the perfect sort of sweater to wear when you were writing your second novel in the last week of September.

Cerulean, Ellie wrote down, her pen making a satisfying scratch on the paper. *A shade of deep blue.*

Sentence: As we stood on the beach, we looked out on the cerulean-blue ocean.

But what should her new novel be about? When she'd started *Hermione Granger, Fifth-Grade Muggle* in June, she'd known exactly what she wanted to write. J. K. Rowling had barely said anything in the Harry Potter books about Hermione's pre-Hogwarts years, and Ellie was dying to know what she'd been like before the books started. When had Hermione discovered she had magical powers? Was she always the smartest one in her class? Did she have any friends? If she did, what kind of friends were they? Good friends, or the kind of friends who turned on you? When Ellie realized she might never know the answers to these questions unless she made them up herself, she'd started writing.

Paradigm, Ellie wrote now. *An example or pattern of something. Sentence: I could write a book about how Lila Willis is a paradigm of a terrible friend.*

Ellie glanced up from her desk. Lila was in the book nook with Rosie Nichols, passing a notebook back and forth. Ellie could just imagine what they were writing about—who liked who, who liked someone who didn't like them back, who was best-looking, who was worst-looking. After school, they'd send out a series of group texts to everyone in Mrs. Herrera's class with all the information they'd compiled. If Ellie made one of their lists, it was usually the biggest geek list. She was typically number three, after Stefan Morrisey and Ben McPherson, although sometimes she nosed ahead of Ben into the number two slot.

It was hard to believe that at the very beginning of school she and Lila had been friends. Well, sort of friends. They'd both been new, although Ellie was used to being new. Up until that summer, her father had been an army lawyer, and her family had moved every two or three years—Texas; Kansas; Washington, DC; even Germany. Then last spring her parents decided they were ready to settle down. They moved to Milton Falls and bought an old house with a big front porch two blocks from downtown, and Ellie's dad opened up his own law office and became the sort of lawyer who helped businesses get set up.

Every morning last summer, Ellie woke up, got

dressed, ate a bowl of cereal, and then waited on her front porch for someone her age to walk by so she could make friends with them. She was good at making friends. She'd been doing it all her life. But no kids walked by, and when Ellie started exploring her neighborhood, she didn't find many kids there, either. There were old people and there were young people with babies. One of the moms with a baby told Ellie that most of the families with kids Ellie's age lived in another part of town, where there were more soccer fields and youth activities.

So Ellie couldn't wait for new-student orientation, which took place a week before school started. She'd finally get a chance to make some friends. And sure enough, after the principal gave a talk about what a great school Milton Falls Middle School was and how every student mattered, all eight hundred of them, a girl came up to Ellie and said, "Are you in sixth grade too? You look like you're in sixth grade."

Ellie had never had a friend like Lila Willis before. Lila was the kind of friend who called her up every night to talk about what they should wear the first day of school and if their outfits should match exactly or just have the same theme. "Maybe patriotic?" Lila had asked the night before her mom was going to take them to the mall to go clothes shopping. "You know, red, white, and blue, maybe with star earrings?"

"I don't have pierced ears," Ellie had told her. "I'm not allowed until I'm twelve. My mom's really old-fashioned."

"You can get your ears pierced at the mall tomorrow," Lila said. "And then you can tell your mom you thought she meant sixth grade."

"I can't do that," Ellie said. "I don't want to lie to my mom."

"Everybody lies to their moms," Lila said. "Like, when my mom asks me how long I've been watching Netflix, I always say 'about twenty minutes,' even though it's been two hours. She always believes me."

They'd ended up getting matching T-shirts in different colors—pink for Lila, purple for Ellie—and white shorts. Instead of earrings, they got matching necklaces with blue butterflies on them. Sitting in the back seat of Mrs. Willis's car on the way home from the mall, they'd taken their outfits out and admired them. "You know what I just thought of?" Lila asked, and Ellie had shaken her head. "Our clothes match and our names sort of match too—Lila and Ellie. I think we're going to make an amazing first-day impression!"

Ellie guessed that was a good thing to do. Mostly she was glad to have a friend to sit with at lunch on the first day and to play with during recess. She bet it wouldn't take long for her and Lila to make friends with other girls. In a way, Ellie thought, everyone in the sixth-grade class was new. This was the first year of middle school for all of them.

The two prettiest sixth-grade girls, Rosie Nichols and Petra Wilde, kept to themselves the first two weeks of school, while other girls hovered nearby and looked for opportunities to offer a Kit Kat bar or a compliment. "Rosie and Petra think they're so special," Lila had sneered. "Let's ignore them." Ellie thought that was funny. How could you ignore someone who was ignoring you first? But she was happy that Lila didn't seem interested in being popular. Ellie just wished she'd been interested in something, well, interesting.

Like watching *Doctor Who* or reading fantasy novels or anything besides looking at fashion magazines and critiquing the models.

The third week of school, Rosie and Petra sat down at Ellie and Lila's lunch table and started asking Lila questions. What were the boys like at your old school? Where did you get that bracelet? Can you teach us to do our hair like yours?

And just like that, Lila was gone. No more phone calls about matching outfits, no more trading lunches, no more Friday night sleepovers, of which they'd had three and had been planning a fourth. On the one hand, Ellie couldn't say that she was that sad about losing Lila, but on the other hand, her feelings were hurt. She'd never been dumped by a friend before, even a friend she wasn't sure she liked all that much.

Once Rosie and Petra had made their pick, the other girls found their groups. Except for Ellie. The girl who was famous for making friends was friendless. She'd approached Aadita Amrit, but Aadita was so shy it was hard to make conversation. Cammi Lovett seemed like someone Ellie would get along with, but

Cammi was joined at the hip with Becca Hobbes, best friends since preschool, apparently.

She'd even tried to make friends with Sam Hawkins, a boy who mostly kept to himself but had interesting habits. Sam carried a small notebook and a pencil in his back pocket, and Ellie had seen him taking notes at odd times—in the cafeteria line at lunch, in the hallway on the way to the media center. She thought that she and Sam probably had a lot in common, but when Ellie tried to talk to him, he just gave her a strange look and walked away. Last week, after Sam had missed three days of class in a row, Mrs. Herrera announced that his family had relocated—Ellie had thought "relocated" was an odd word to use; why not just say they'd moved?—and he was now going to another school. One less person to reject her, Ellie had thought, and permanently marked Sam Hawkins off her list of potential friends.

After a while, Ellie gave up trying to make new friends. She wasn't that lonely, not really, and she had her writing career to attend to.

Autodidact, she wrote in her spelling notebook. *A*

self-taught person. Sentence: When it comes to being a novelist, I am an autodidact.

Maybe her new novel should be about Mrs. Herrera's homeroom class. They spent most of their day together, traveling from classroom to classroom, after all, and Mrs. Herrera always said to write about what you know. Ellie got so excited by that idea that she pushed too hard on her pen and ink splattered across her definitions. That was okay; Mrs. Herrera wouldn't mind. She liked Ellie's fountain pen. "I remember using one of those in high school," she'd told Ellie one day at recess, when Ellie had stayed inside to help grade spelling tests. "I don't know where I got the idea. From reading novels, I guess."

That's when Ellie had known Mrs. Herrera would be her favorite teacher of all time. She was a teacher who understood about fountain pens and how a good book could make you do things you'd never thought about doing before. Like write your own book. And then write another one.

Ellie had never had a teacher like Mrs. Herrera before, a teacher who seemed like an actual person you could imagine sitting on her living room couch at night reading a book or petting her cat. Maybe it was because of Mrs. Herrera's shelf, the one by her desk where she kept her special collection of special things. "These are the things that remind me of who I am and why I'm here," Mrs. Herrera had explained to the class on the first day of school. "Some days teaching is hard, and sometimes I feel tired or unmotivated. My special collection of special things helps me remember that life is interesting and learning is good and teaching is a noble profession."

Some of the items in Mrs. Herrera's collection were so personal that they didn't mean much to Ellie. There was a small, framed photograph of Mrs. Herrera's favorite teacher ever, for instance, the one who inspired her to become a teacher herself, and there was a key to her first apartment, which was her first experience of independence and freedom. Ellie understood why they were special to Mrs. Herrera; they just weren't special to Ellie.

What Ellie loved best was a small blue bowl filled with sugar cubes from all the wonderful places Mrs. Herrera had had high tea: the Savoy in London, Angelina's in Paris, and the Plaza Hotel in New York. Ellie had only heard of the Plaza (because of *Eloise*), and she wasn't exactly sure what high tea was as opposed to regular tea, but she loved the paper-wrapped cubes of sugar so much she had to stuff her hands in her pockets whenever she was near Mrs. Herrera's special collection so she wouldn't snatch one and run away with it.

Ellie understood the importance of having special things. She had special pens and special notebooks, and she never mixed them up, never used her drawing pen for writing, never wrote spelling words in her art journal. Now she put away her spelling notebook and took out the notebook she only used to write stories and poems in. On the top of the first blank page, she printed *The Class* in her neatest cursive. And then she started to write.

Chapter Two

Becca

Friday, September 29

On Monday Mrs. Herrera had promised her home-room class a pizza lunch on Friday if they could read a total of a thousand pages by the end of the week. Becca thought that when you had someone like Stefan Morrisey in your class, a boy who read one two-pound book per day, a thousand pages was no problem at all. When she pointed this out to Mrs. Herrera, however, several of her classmates had tried to shut her up. But who wanted easy pizza?

Anyway, Becca herself could easily read at least two books between Monday and Friday, so Mrs. Herrera doubled the number of pages. The class, which included two other star readers (Ellie Barker and Ben McPherson), still met the goal easily, and so at eleven fifteen Friday morning, Mrs. Herrera put in the order.

Thirty minutes later, the pizzas were lined up on the long table at the back of the room, and Becca almost fainted, they smelled so good. But when Mrs. Herrera opened up the boxes, she discovered the pizza place had gotten the order wrong.

"Instead of three large pepperonis and two large cheeses, they brought four extra-large pepperonis and one small cheese," Mrs. Herrera said as she examined the pizzas. She turned to look at the class. "Everybody but Aadita eats pepperoni, right?" she asked, and everyone nodded.

But then Carson Bennett, the most popular boy in their class, raised his hand and said, "My mom won't let me eat pepperoni anymore because of the nitrates. Or nitrites. I'm not quite sure. Besides, I'm thinking about becoming a vegetarian."

Aadita's face lit up with a shy smile. She had been the class's only vegetarian up to now, and Becca could tell she wouldn't mind some company.

Becca's hand shot up. She had no idea how it happened. She hadn't meant to raise her hand. She loved pepperoni. But when Mrs. Herrera said, "Yes, Becca? Do you not eat pepperoni?" Becca had shaken her head. "I can't. I'm a vegetarian too."

Her best friend, Cammi, raised her hand (in Mrs. Herrera's class you always raised your hand, even when you were discussing pizza, and even if your question was for someone other than Mrs. Herrera). "Since when are you a vegetarian? You had a turkey sandwich for lunch yesterday."

"I decided last night," Becca said, and she said it with so much conviction that she almost believed it herself. "I saw a documentary about how farm animals are treated. It was pretty horrible." She turned to Carson. "I think it's great you're a vegetarian too."

Carson ignored her. Boys like Carson usually ignored her, but Becca hadn't really cared about it until this year. Suddenly, and much to her dismay, she cared a lot. She had been trying to figure out how to get Carson's attention since school started, but so far none of her ideas had worked. He hadn't wanted to be her study buddy in history, even though Becca was excellent at history and

Carson had a hard time getting Cs, even on the easy stuff like the Friday quizzes. She made a funny video of her dog, Biggley, and tried to make Carson watch it on her phone, but he'd just given her a confused look and said, "Why would I want to watch *that?*"

Becca raised her hand. "Mrs. Herrera, since one thing Carson is worried about is nitrates, he should definitely eat the cheese pizza. I'll be happy to share it with him."

"What about Aadita?" Mrs. Herrera asked. "Up until just now, she was the only official vegetarian in this class. Suddenly I have three."

Becca could tell Mrs. Herrera wasn't happy with her. She was pretty sure Mrs. Herrera knew she was lying about being a vegetarian. Becca felt a little sick. She'd been working so hard to make Mrs. Herrera like her, and now she'd blown it! Over a stupid pizza. Becca blinked back tears. Five weeks' worth of hard work, down the drain. And now Mrs. Herrera would probably call Becca's mom. *Becca caused a commotion in class today,* she'd say. *I'm very disappointed.*

Becca's stomach started to hurt. She'd never had a teacher disappointed in her before. She didn't even know that was possible.

* * *

Up until sixth grade, Becca Hobbes had always been her teachers' favorite. It really wasn't that hard; in fact, it just took a few simple tricks. First, never talk back or talk when the teacher is talking. Second, always do your homework and turn it in on time. Third, make sure to compliment your teacher twice a day, once in the morning and again when the last bell rings and you're walking out the classroom door.

People called her a brownnoser or a Goody Two-shoes, but Becca ignored them. She knew it was her job to keep the adults in her life happy, and she was very, very good at it. She was good at bringing her mother a cup of tea in the morning and listening sympathetically as she complained about how early Becca's father got up in the morning and how late he came home at night, and how she had a headache again and needed more sleep. Becca was good at helping her little sister get ready for school and cleaning up the breakfast dishes so that her mother wouldn't lecture her when she got home about how mothers weren't servants, they were people too, and everyone needed to do their fair share around the house. She was good at leaving a few minutes early in the morning to fetch Mrs. Quentin's paper from the bottom of her driveway and deliver it to the elderly woman's front porch before she walked to the bus stop. She knew that when Mrs. Quentin saw Becca's mother, she'd gush about what a nice, thoughtful girl Becca was, and that would make Becca's mother happy.

Becca's life was about keeping adults happy. And when Becca was at school, that meant it was all about keeping the teachers happy.

It was easy enough to do, especially because Becca usually got 100s on her tests and quizzes and liked to volunteer in class when nobody else would. She was eager to be the first one to give her oral report or to miss five minutes of recess when a teacher needed someone to erase the whiteboards or straighten up the reading center. As a result, her teachers had always loved her and said things like, "I wish more of my students were like Becca Hobbes."

And sometimes they even e-mailed her mother telling her what a good girl she was, and that made her mother happy, which made life a whole lot easier for Becca.

Mrs. Herrera was different. Mrs. Herrera didn't seem to have a favorite student. Becca had been working on her steadily since the beginning of school, paying her three compliments a day rather than her usual two and bringing in special treats that she left on Mrs. Herrera's desk—pencils that read WORLD'S GREATEST TEACHER and bags of mini Oreos. She stuck Post-it notes on the treats that said things like, *This is for all the hard work you do! xoxo, Becca.* Mrs. Herrera always thanked her, but she still didn't act like Becca was her favorite. She'd never e-mailed Becca's mother to say how much she appreciated Becca's efforts and her thoughtful gifts.

Up until the pizza party, Becca had refused to give up. In fact, she thought she might be making progress. Mrs. Herrera had twice asked her to run up to the office to drop off some forms in the last two weeks, and last week she had complimented Becca on how neat she kept her language arts notebook. Becca was already planning what to get Mrs. Herrera for Christmas, something her teacher would love so much she'd put it in her special collection of special things, next to her signed copy of *Hatchet* and her grandmother's tortoiseshell comb. She was pretty sure a really good Christmas present would clinch the deal.

Well, she'd have to come up with an entirely new game plan, Becca thought now, sniffing back her tears. But first she needed to solve the pizza problem.

"Aadita can have pepperoni and just take the pepperonis off. In her culture, cows are holy, but pigs aren't, so it's okay if there's pepperoni juice on her pizza," she told Mrs. Herrera. "Personally, now that I'm a vegetarian like Carson, pepperoni juice would probably make me throw up. I mean, you could even wipe the juice off with a napkin and I'd still get sick to my stomach."

She turned and smiled at Carson, but Carson didn't smile back.

Cammi raised her hand again. "Could you please stop saying 'pepperoni juice'? I'm losing my appetite."

A bunch of other people said they were losing their appetites too, and Lila Willis said she'd just remembered she'd seen the same animal documentary that Becca had seen and now she didn't want to eat meat anymore either. Lila was one of the three really popular girls in their class, and in Becca's opinion she was almost as mean as Petra Wilde, but that didn't stop Carson from giving her a big smile and saying, "Way to join the team, Lila!" Something he had definitely not said to Becca.

As soon as Lila said she didn't want pepperoni, no one else wanted it either, except for Ben McPherson, who never cared what other kids did. "Is it okay if I start?" he asked Mrs. Herrera, who nodded. "Who else will eat some pepperoni?" she asked the class, and when no one else said they would, she looked irritated. "Well, I just wasted a lot of our special treat money," she said. "You might have become vegetarians *before* I placed our order."

Aadita raised her hand. "I'll eat pepperoni if I can take off the pepperonis," she offered. "I think that would be okay."

Carson raised his hand. "Maybe I could have pepperoni without the pepperoni too. I could use a napkin to sort of clean the pizza up."

Everyone decided to have pepperoni pizza without the pepperoni. Becca wanted a piece of pepperoni pizza so badly she thought she might fall over, but now she couldn't have one, even if she took the pepperoni off and wiped the pizza off with a napkin.

"I'll just skip lunch," she told Mrs. Herrera, hoping her teacher would notice the great sacrifice she was making for the class. "Carson and Aadita can have the cheese pizza. Could I go to the book nook? I can alphabetize the books while everyone else is eating."

"I have some things you could eat," Mrs. Herrera said, opening her bottom desk drawer. "Here's an apple and some cheese crackers. Oh, and three packs of mini Oreos."

They were the same packs of mini Oreos that Becca had given her. One still even had Becca's Post-it note on it.

It was the sight of all those uneaten Oreos that made Becca realize she would never be Mrs. Herrera's favorite. Mrs. Herrera would never e-mail her mother to say she wished all her students were just like Becca Hobbes. Becca's mother would want to know if Becca had started misbehaving in class. Was Becca turning into Leda French, a girl on their street who'd dyed her hair blue and started wearing clunky black boots in ninth grade?

Seeing those cookies made Becca realize that Mrs. Herrera wasn't a very nice person. A nice person would have at least taken the Oreos to the teacher's lounge and let Becca think that she'd eaten them. Mrs. Herrera just left the packs of cookies—one with Becca's note still attached!—where anyone could see them. It was humiliating.

A nice person would have e-mailed Becca's mother by now.

That was when Becca changed her plan. Now you couldn't pay Becca enough to be Mrs. Herrera's favorite. From now on, she would be Mrs. Herrera's unfavorite. She would make Mrs. Herrera pay.

Chapter Three

Carson

Friday, September 29

Carson Bennett didn't get excited about the grocery bags stacked in the minivan's wayback when his mom picked him up from school on Friday afternoon. He knew there wasn't anything good in them. In July Carson's mom had decided to become a vegan, which meant they all sort of became vegans. Being a vegan meant they didn't eat meat or cheese or anything made with milk or anything that came from any part of an animal. No processed foods. Carson and his brother were allowed to eat cheese pizza at parties, but she made them promise that they would never, ever eat pepperoni or anything else that had nitrates or nitrites, which were some of the worst things they could put in their bodies.

A year ago he would have complained, but now Carson didn't complain about anything.

A year ago most of the stuff his mom bought at the grocery store was healthy, because she believed in eating healthy meals all through the week, lots of vegetables, no junk. But she'd also believed in loosening up a little on weekends, so after Carson and Win carried the bags of groceries into the house when they got home, they dug down through the broccoli and chicken breasts and brown rice to find the good stuff, Cokes and Nutty Buddy ice-cream cones (six to a box, so three for Carson, three for Win) and one pack of Double Stuf Oreos and two bags of ranch-flavored Doritos.

A year ago, weekends had been about pigging out and playing soccer and going to Frankie's Fun House with their friends. Carson's dad traveled a lot during the week, so he mostly liked to chill on Saturday and Sunday, which was fine; his mom was willing to drive them all over the place, mall, movies, games, it didn't matter. "Where do you want to go now?" she'd ask, jangling her car keys.

They always ended up someplace good.

Then Carson's mom got cancer. One day she was fine, and the next day she was in the hospital for surgery. After that, she had chemo, lots and lots of chemo, and she lost her hair and her energy and her appetite. Grammy came to stay with them, and Carson's dad was home a lot more, but there were no more Friday night movies at the mall or Sunday afternoons spent at Frankie's Fun House, no more jangling car keys.

Mostly Carson and Win spent the summer riding their bikes to the neighborhood pool. Their buddies lived in different neighborhoods and went to different pools, so the neighborhood pool was pretty boring, but what else were they supposed to do? Home was too depressing, and besides, they had to be quiet because their mom was always resting. At the pool Carson and Win did a lot of underwater fighting, which was sort of fun, except for the last time, when they'd ended up grabbing each other's hair and pulling really hard, and when they came up out of the water, they both were crying, the big hiccuping-snorting sort of crying, snot coming out of their noses, and they never did any more underwater fighting after that.

In July and August the blood tests came back cancer-free three times in a row, and now his mom's hair was growing in and she felt a lot better, though she still had to go to the doctor's every month to get her blood checked. Hers was the kind of cancer that could come back. If it didn't reappear for three years, the doctors said, it probably never would, but three years was a long time from now.

"How did the pizza party go?" his mom asked as she pulled away from the pickup line. "Was there plenty of cheese?"

"Yeah," Carson said. "I had three pieces."

"Good," his mom said, sounding distracted as she waited to make a left-hand turn out of the school parking lot. "By the way, I got a call from somebody's mother today, but now I've got total chemo brain and can't think who it was. A girl in your class is having a birthday party tomorrow afternoon at her house, but the mom is just inviting kids now so the kids who aren't being invited wouldn't hear about it. Does that strike you as strange?"

Carson's mom glanced over at him. He'd noticed lately that she'd started talking to him like he was almost grown up, asking his opinion about stuff, telling him more personal things about herself. He didn't really like it, but it didn't matter what he liked or didn't like anymore. *Our primary goal is to make your mother happy,* his dad had said back in May, and as far as Carson knew, that was still true.

"They'll hear about it Monday," Carson said, "So it doesn't really make any difference."

"Lila!" his mom exclaimed suddenly. "The girl having the party is Lila, and her mother's name is . . . Well, I'm not going to remember that. But she said the party is at four o'clock, it's a cookout, and instead of a present you're supposed to bring a book for the Book Harvest program. And your swim stuff, because it's a pool party. Do you think it's a little late for a pool party? Maybe it's a global warming thing—pool parties all year round, why not?"

His mom sounded happy and relieved because she remembered the message, but Carson didn't feel happy or relieved. He didn't want to go to a party, not even a pool party at Lila Willis's house. Nothing against Lila personally; he thought it was cool how she'd said she was a vegetarian in class today, like she wanted to make him feel less dumb about saying he couldn't have pepperoni. But he'd been to one other birthday party since school started—Garrison's birthday party at Climb the Walls climbing center—and he'd felt strange the whole time. He could tell nobody else there had a mom who'd had cancer; if they did, they wouldn't be acting like everything was so great.

"Did you say it's a cookout?" Carson asked his mom now. "That means hamburgers and hot dogs, right? On a grill?"

His mom frowned. "Yeah, usually."

"You said no grilled stuff. Grilled equals car—" He couldn't think of the word, but he knew it meant stuff that caused cancer.

"Carcinogens," his mom said. "And grilled stuff can be okay, just as long as it's not charred."

"But hot dogs aren't okay," Carson reminded her. "Hot dogs are the worst."

"You could bring some tofu dogs. You liked the ones I got last week, right—the spicy ones?"

"Really, Mom? You really want me to walk into a party with tofu dogs?"

"Why not? I bet at least one or two of the kids will be vegetarians. They'll appreciate that somebody thought of it."

He didn't bother to tell her that everyone in his class was now a vegetarian. It was kind of cool, how between him and Lila, they'd gotten the whole class turned against meat. Stuff like that had started happening to him last year. He hadn't noticed it at first, and then Stefan Morrisey, who was his math partner, pointed it out to him one day. "Before Christmas all the boys in our class wore white footie socks, and then after Christmas, after you started wearing those socks like soccer players wear? A week later everyone else was wearing them too."

Now things like that happened all the time. Carson didn't know why exactly, but he had to admit there were some pretty cool things about it. People gave you the good junk from their lunches, their M&M's and cupcakes and Fritos. Girls like Becca Hobbes let him copy their homework, although he tried not to ask Becca too often because she got so freaked out about getting caught. "I'm only doing this because we're friends," she'd say, looking nervously around. As far as Carson was concerned, they weren't friends at all, not that he ever said so.

All in all, sixth grade was pretty okay. His mom wasn't sick, people gave him things he didn't even have to ask for, and for once in his life he had a teacher who seemed to like him. Not only that, Mrs. Herrera liked soccer and football, too, which was sort of amazing, since those were his sports. On that shelf where she kept all that stuff she liked, she had a miniature Browns football signed by this old-time player named Jim Brown, and once when Carson had to stay in at lunch because he'd gotten a little rowdy during morning announcements, out of nowhere she'd called, "Go out for a pass, Carson!" and thrown him the ball. And she'd even caught it when he threw it back. Pretty cool.

"Doesn't Win have a game tomorrow at four?" Carson asked his mom, thinking about everyone at the party tomorrow throwing balls around and splashing each other in the water, laughing and sort of being jerks (he could already hear Matt Collins yelling, "Take a joke, dude!" which is what he always said after he'd done something really stupid and mean). "We kind of have a pact about going to each other's games."

They were at a red light. His mom turned to look at him. "Carson, you know Win won't mind if you miss a game. Besides, he's got another one on Sunday."

"We have a *pact*, Mom," Carson said. "Do you understand what the word 'pact' means?"

He couldn't look at her. He looked out the window instead, and it took him a second to realize that he was crying. His mom could never understand what it was like spending the whole summer underwater, kicking and punching his brother, his brother's slow-motion fists and feet kicking and punching back, how terrible and great that had felt. Every single day all summer they'd pretended to try to kill each other. It was like Carson was the cancer and Win was the cancer and if they just hit and kicked each other hard enough, the cancer would go away.

And it had. His mom's cancer had gone away. But it could come back any minute. If Carson or Win let down their guards—broke their promises, ate pepperoni, stepped outside the force field holding their family together the way the water had held Carson and his brother together this summer—the cancer could come back.

"I know what a pact is," his mom said softly. She reached over and put her hand on Carson's shoulder, and then the light turned green and they headed for the elementary school, which was just a block down the street. When they got there, Win was waiting for them at the curb, and Carson could tell by the look on his face that something was up.

"Hey, fart face," Win said as he slid into the minivan's back seat. "Do you know that in Spanish, 'Carson' is the word for 'butt ugly'?"

"News to me," Carson replied, turning around to look at his brother. "Did you know that 'Win' means 'fifth-grade snot eater'?"

Win wiggled his eyebrows and opened his backpack so that Carson could see inside to where two bags of Cool Ranch Doritos were nestled against each other.

"You're a green-bean snorter," Carson said, grinning at his brother.

"You're a cockroach chewer," Win replied.

"I was thinking we could have some quinoa and strawberries for snack when we get home," his mother said, and that made Carson and Win laugh so hard that Carson thought his guts might explode all over the car.

"Yeah, Mom," Win said. "Sounds delish."

Carson shot his brother a thumbs-up. "Sounds like the best thing ever."

Chapter Four

Cammi

Saturday, September 30

When Cammi Lovett got up on Saturday morning, she went to the bathroom and brushed her teeth, and then she went downstairs to watch Netflix on the computer. On Saturdays the screen rules were different. She could have an hour of screen time in the morning and an hour in the afternoon, but to get her hour in the afternoon she had to spend an hour reading or exercising first. She had to earn her second hour.

Cammi had her own weekend screen rules. If she got up before her parents—which she almost always did— she had free screen time until one of them woke up.

It seemed like a fair rule to her, although she couldn't quite say why. She could also eat as many cookies as she wanted, because if her parents didn't see the cookies, then the cookies didn't exist.

While Netflix was loading up, she checked her phone for texts. There were three from Becca sent this morning, the first one at six thirty a.m. Becca made a big deal about getting up early every day, not just school days. It was part of her program for Building a Better Becca, which she had started at the beginning of last summer. At first Cammi had sort of liked the idea. For her birthday in May, she'd been given a subscription to *Girls' Life* magazine, and reading the articles had made her realize that she was behind in all sorts of things, like knowing what kind of jeans she looked best in and how to moisturize (you needed different products for your face and the rest of your body, it turned out, and it was important to moisturize your hair, too).

The only problem with building a better Cammi? It was boring. Moisturizing was extremely boring, and so was reading about the do's and don't's of breaking up (she'd never even had a boyfriend!) and going shopping for the shoes that would make her shine. All the shoes in the pictures had high heels, which Cammi thought was crazy. Where was she going to wear high heels? The Oscars?

But the most boring thing of all was listening to Becca go on and on about her plan to impress for success. That was the motto for her Building a Better Becca (and a better Cammi) program. Becca believed that when you worked hard to impress other people, you were destined to be successful. By mid-July Cammi had started asking her, "Successful at what? Why do we have to be successful? We're only eleven." Becca swatted all of Cammi's questions away. "Just stick with me and you'll see," she'd said.

Of course Cammi had stuck with Becca. Who else was she supposed to stick with? They lived in the same neighborhood, went to the same pool, rode the same bus to school, were in the same grade, and this year they both had Mrs. Herrera for their lead teacher. It was like they were living the exact same lives.

Except that they weren't. For one thing, here it was eight forty-five and Cammi was just getting up. Plus, she was going to watch *One Tree Hill* on Netflix, a show that Becca disapproved of because it was junky, even if it was from a million years ago. That was one of Becca's mom's words. *Junky.* As in "a bunch of junk." As in "a big waste of time." But what was wrong with wasting time every once in a while? Or eating Chips Ahoy cookies for breakfast on Saturday mornings?

Cammi scrolled through Becca's texts. **Need to plan the Carson campaign,** she'd written in the first one. Cammi rolled her eyes when she read this. Carson Bennett was the cutest, most popular boy in their class. To him, girls like Becca and Cammi were bugs on the windshield of life. But for some reason, Becca thought she had a chance to become Carson's girlfriend or even just his friend. **Why don't you come over at 10?** the next text, sent at 6:59, read. In her last text, Becca's plans get specific. **Bring your GL mags with you. We can make a scrapbook for stuff like clothes and what to do with our hair. I bought some makeup at Target yesterday, so we could experiment as long as we wash everything off before my mom sees.**

Cammi wondered how Becca managed to buy makeup without her mom noticing. Well, that was the funny thing about Becca's mom, she thought. Either Mrs. Hobbes was totally on Becca's case for the littlest things ("Becca, I see three hairs in the bathroom sink, and they look like yours!") or she was kind of weirdly absent. She was also the only mom Cammi knew who drank wine at lunch or took long afternoon naps. "Her grandmother was from Europe," Becca liked to say whenever there was an open wine bottle on the kitchen counter in the middle of the day or they found her mom asleep on the couch. When they'd been little, Cammi had accepted that as a reasonable explanation. Now she'd seen enough movies and watched enough TV to think *Riiiiight* whenever Becca used some ancient European relative to explain her mom's strange behavior.

Cammi heard the upstairs toilet flush and scrambled to shut down the computer. She pulled her copy of *Wonder* out of her backpack and opened to a random page. They were reading *Wonder* in LA, and Cammi thought you could tell a lot about people by how they reacted to it. Henry Lloyd had brought in pictures of people with the main character's condition he'd printed out from the Internet, and a lot of the boys had started yelling stuff like, "Dude, how rude is that?" and "Who puked up that face?"

Bart Weems had looked at the pictures and shaken his head. "If we weren't reading *Wonder*, I'd be totally grossed out," he'd said. "But if I pretend these are pictures of Auggie, they don't bother me so much."

Cammi had wanted to go up to Bart Weems and shake his hand, but unfortunately, Bart chewed his fingernails and his fingertips always looked water-logged and mushroom-y, so Cammi didn't actually want to touch them. Maybe she could write about that for the journal entry she was supposed to do for LA this weekend. She wouldn't use Bart's name, of course. But she could write about how you could like someone and see that they were a great person but still sort of be grossed out by them. She knew it wasn't the nicest thing in the world to admit, but she felt like Mrs. Herrera would understand.

Her phone buzzed. Cammi didn't have to look to know it was Becca. She sighed. No offense, but she was starting to think it was time to take a Becca break. Her entire life, Becca had been making plans and Cammi had been following them. Some of Becca's ideas over the years had been great—the lemonade stand they'd had this summer, where they made enough money to buy matching phone cases—and others had flopped big-time, like when they set up a sidewalk beauty parlor and dyed Flora Foote's hair with cherry-flavored Kool-Aid. Good or bad, interesting or really stupid, Cammi always ended up going along with Becca's plans because—because why? Because that was her role in life, she guessed. Because Becca pushed and pushed and pushed until it was just easier to say yes to whatever scheme she'd come up with than to resist.

But this whole Carson Bennett campaign might be where Cammi finally put her foot down. Really, she was supposed to help Becca find ways to make Carson fall in love with her? Come *on*. Why couldn't Becca see that boys like Carson didn't like girls like Becca and Cammi?

Or maybe he just didn't like girls like Becca. Had Cammi ever considered that?

She fell back as though the force of this idea had pushed her into the couch cushions. Did she actually have any evidence that Carson Bennett didn't like her? Not *like* like, but like as in "didn't actually find her all that irritating" or "had friendly feelings about her." Last year they'd done a Spanish project together and gotten a B-, which was not a great grade for Cammi, but Carson had high-fived her and yelled, "All right, pardnah!" (This was something Carson could get away with, saying "pardnah" instead of "partner," even if it was super dumb. If someone like Bart Weems had said it, the whole class would have gone quiet until someone started snickering behind their hand, and then everyone would have laughed until they were rolling out of their seats.)

Maybe she should text Carson, just to say hi. She wouldn't say anything stupid (definitely not Hi, pardnah! or even Hi, partner!). She could text something like Hey, have you studied for the Spanish quiz on Tuesday? It was the sort of question that didn't have any secret meaning, and it wouldn't be a big deal if their conversation didn't go anywhere. She could just act like she was trying to figure out how much time she should spend on getting ready for the test.

Cammi had to admit that it felt a little disloyal to text Carson, especially since she was totally ignoring Becca. Carson was Becca's crush, not hers. But she wasn't trying to get Carson to like her, not *like her* like her. She just wanted to see if Carson saw her as someone separate from Becca Hobbes. Someone who was kind of normal and fun and maybe even had her own plans and ideas. *Good* plans and ideas.

She could hear her dad in the kitchen, making coffee. She didn't want to text Carson in front of him, so she slipped her phone into her back pocket and tiptoed out of the family room and up the stairs. Technically, she wasn't supposed to have her phone in her bedroom, but technically, only her mom remembered to check and her mom was still asleep.

Her room was a mess, something she'd deal with after she sent Carson a text. It would keep her mind off waiting for him to text back. But wait—what if he didn't text back? Then what?

Then nothing, she decided. It wasn't like he'd come up to her in homeroom on Monday and say, *Hey, I got your text but I decided not to reply because you're a big social zero.* If Carson didn't text back, Cammi would just pretend she'd never sent a text in the first place. No biggie.

She pulled her phone out of her pocket and flopped down on her unmade bed. Carson was already in her contact list, because Becca had decided they should have all the popular people's numbers in their contact lists. That way, if Carson or Petra or Garrison ever texted one of them, they wouldn't have to text back, Who is this?

Hi, this is Cammi. Are you going to study for the Spanish quiz this weekend, she wrote, her heart pounding so hard she could feel it in her ears, or are you going to wait until Monday night.

She tapped send and then realized with horror she had put a period instead of a question mark at the end of the sentence. Would Carson think she was an idiot? *Okay,* she told herself, *take a breath and calm down.* What was the likelihood that someone like Carson Bennett would even notice? He wasn't Ben McPherson, after all, Mr. Brainiac of the universe. To be honest, Cammi wasn't even sure Carson was smart.

She was kicking the clothes on the floor into a pile when her phone pinged. Barely thirty seconds had passed since she'd sent the text. Cammi's hands started shaking. Had Carson Bennett really replied that fast? No, it was probably Becca again. Cammi sighed and rolled her eyes. Why couldn't Becca go five minutes without sending her a text? Could she be any more annoying?

But when she picked up her phone, the name at the top of the screen wasn't Becca's. It was Carson's.

Carson Bennett had texted her back.

Carson. Bennett.

Yeah, I got a D on the last test and my moms really made, he'd written. You want to come over tomorrow and study? Unless you got a D too!

Cammi took a deep breath. This could be a prank. She could say yes and Carson might text, You thought I was serious? He could be hanging out with his friends—his pardnahs—and they might all be laughing hysterically right this very minute. Still, what choice did Cammi have?

Yeah, that sounds good, she wrote. What time?

She squeezed her eyes shut. Took another deep breath. Waited.

How about after lunch? Maybe like 1?

Cool, Cammi texted back. See you then.

Cool. C YA!

Cammi stared at her phone. Was this really happening? She took a screenshot and was about to send it to Becca, but then she thought better of it. Becca would insist on coming over and planning what Cammi should wear and forcing her to brainstorm a list of ten conversation starters. She'd want to plot out a strategy for getting Carson to ask Cammi to the Fall Ball. She'd probably want to dye Cammi's hair with cherry-flavored Kool-Aid. She'd probably ask to come along. No, Cammi decided. She'd better keep Becca out of this.

She clicked on Becca's last text. Sorry, she wrote. I'm not feeling so good. My mom says I better stay home this weekend.

Then she fell back against her pillow and started to laugh. She was going over to Carson Bennett's house tomorrow! Where next? The White House? Buckingham Palace?

Carson Bennett's house? Cammi sat up straight. What if she went over there and said stupid things and Carson ended up hating her? *Okay, don't panic,* she thought. *Carson likes sports. You like sports. You could talk about how cool it is that Mrs. Herrera has a football signed by Jim Brown.* Cammi hadn't actually known who Jim Brown was until she asked her dad, who told her he had been a running back for Cleveland in the 1960s and was one of the greatest football players ever. Maybe Cammi could spend time this afternoon doing some research on Jim Brown and use it as a conversation starter. *So I guess you probably know all about Jim Brown,* she'd say casually, and if Carson said no, he didn't really know all that much, then Cammi could impress him with her extensive Jim Brown knowledge.

Down the hall, the toilet flushed in her parents' bathroom. Cammi scrambled out of bed, shoving her phone in her pocket. Her mom was up. Time to go downstairs and restart her morning. She grabbed the September *Girls' Life* on the way out of her room. A little football talk, some lip gloss . . . Tomorrow could be a very interesting day.

Chapter Five

Ben

Sunday, October 1

When Ben's mom knocked on his door Sunday morning, Ben pretended to be asleep, even after she'd peeked into his room and said, "Ben? Honey? Are you up? Because I'm leaving for church in thirty minutes, and I'd like you to go."

Ben thought about asking if his dad was going, but that was risky. On the one hand, if his mom said no—and Ben knew there was a slightly higher than average chance that she would—then Ben could say, "I'm going to stay home with Dad" and get away with it. His parents were putting a serious emphasis on father-son time now that Ben was about to turn twelve, one year short of becoming a terrible teenager.

But if she said yes, then Ben would have no choice. His best option, he decided, was to pretend to be asleep. His mother would go downstairs, make his sister Sadie breakfast and then braid Sadie's hair, and by the time she remembered to check on Ben again, it would be too late. A year ago she might have made him go anyway, but that was before Ben had started giving a running commentary of the service and Pastor Alamance's sermons. "I'm trying to pray here," his mother would hiss at him. "Prayer is highly unscientific," Ben would whisper back, and she'd smack his knee and ignore him for the rest of church, even as he continued his critique.

As soon as he heard his mother sigh and shut the door, Ben sat up. He took his glasses off his nightstand and put them on, bringing his room into focus. Right now his plan was to stay in bed and read until his mother and Sadie left for church, after which he'd go downstairs and ask his dad to make french toast.

From outside his window came the sound of bottles crashing into a bin. He bet it was Lila Willis's mom emptying out the recycling from the party yesterday. He still couldn't believe his mom had made him go. Why oh why did the Yangs have to move this summer and make their house available to anyone who wanted to buy it? And if they had to move, why did someone like Lila Willis have to move in and make Ben's life miserable?

"You've been invited to a party!" Ben's mother had declared the minute he'd walked in the door on Friday afternoon. "Lila across the street is having a special and supersecret birthday party tomorrow and you're one of the special people she's invited!"

Ben had dropped his backpack on the foyer floor and brushed past his mother on the way to the kitchen. "That doesn't make any sense," he said. "Lila hates me."

"How could she hate you?" his mother chirped. "You're neighbors!"

His mother was always saying things like that. Half the time she made absolutely no sense at all.

"Trust me, Mom," Ben said as he opened the fridge and searched around for something to eat. "Lila Willis does not like me. She thinks I'm a geek. Which, strictly speaking, I am. But in my opinion, being a geek is a good thing. In Lila's opinion, it's the worst thing in the world."

"Then it's up to you to change her opinion!" Ben's mother reached around him and pulled out a bowl of grapes from the refrigerator. "Eat these, honey. Or *something* healthy."

Ben took the bowl of grapes. Maybe that could be their trade-off: he would eat grapes and she would leave him alone.

But no.

"What I don't understand is why Lila would invite you if she didn't like you," his mother said. "That doesn't make sense to me."

Sitting down at the kitchen table, Ben picked up the book he'd been reading that morning and started where he'd left off. Sometimes if he ignored his mother, she'd go back to her office upstairs, with the warning that they were not done with their discussion.

Not today, unfortunately. She sat down at the table across from him and said, "Seriously, Ben. I think it's nice you've been invited to a party. You need to make some new friends now that Justin has moved."

"Stefan is my friend," Ben said. "What's wrong with Stefan?"

"Nothing's wrong with Stefan, but all you boys do is play on the computer."

"We play Settlers of Catan and Risk," Ben pointed out. "And sometimes we play Dungeons and Dragons."

His mother raised an eyebrow. "Yeah, well, I'm not crazy about that."

Ben shrugged and continued to read.

"You still haven't answered my question," his mother insisted. "Why would she invite you if she didn't like you?"

This was the fascinating thing to Ben about his mother: she just couldn't believe that someone might dislike him. The idea that many of his classmates disliked him was incomprehensible to her. Ben didn't have the heart to explain that kids like him and Stefan were just too geeky to fit in, and even more importantly, they didn't want to. Why would he care if Lila or that idiot Carson liked him? They had a combined IQ of three.

He could see from the look on his mom's face that he was going to have to go to Lila's party. There was no getting around it. "Okay, fine, I'll go for an hour," he said with a sigh, ignoring his mom's victorious smile.

At four p.m. on Saturday afternoon, he'd gone across the street with a book for Book Harvest in one hand and a birthday card with a Barnes & Noble gift card in the other. He'd picked a book he'd read at least five times and wouldn't mind reading again at the party. He hoped there was a comfortable lawn chair he could move to the corner of the yard, because that was his party plan: read for an hour and then go home.

The look on Lila's face when she saw him told Ben everything he needed to know. Her mother had made her invite him. "Food's over there," she told him, pointing to a table on the deck. "Pool's there, obviously. We've got extra towels."

"I might swim later," Ben said, which was a big fat lie. He hadn't even brought his suit. "It's a little chilly right now. Did you ever consider that fall is a strange time to have a pool party?"

"Whatever," Lila said, and then ran back to the pool,

yelling, "Watch out, Matt, because I'm going to get you when you're not looking!"

Ben knew exactly where he wanted to hang out. When he and Justin Yang had been in third grade, they'd built a kingdom under the willow tree in the back corner of the yard. They'd called it Willowland, and they ruled it together, organizing their armies against the evil Lion Monster (also known as Justin's cat, Sally, who usually avoided them as much as possible when they were occupying Willowland). By fourth grade, they'd moved inside, into the world of Minecraft, but for a while Ben was obsessed with the world they'd created. He'd even had dreams about it.

Dragging a lawn chair across the lawn, Ben was hardly aware there was a party going on behind him. Third grade was the last time he'd spent much time in Justin's backyard, and now it was all coming back to him, how the air you breathed under the willow tree seemed different from regular air. It was cooler and fresher and somehow more alive.

This wasn't so bad, Ben thought as he settled himself into his chair and opened his book. When he got home he'd have to text Justin, give him the update on Willowland. As far as Ben could tell, things looked pretty much the same. They'd spent most of their time constructing walls out of gravel they'd taken from the walkway out front, and though none of the walls had survived, Ben saw gravel scattered here and there around the willow's roots. Remnants of their kingdom.

He checked his watch and saw that he had fifty-five minutes to go. No problem whatsoever. *Wind howled through the night,* he read in his book, *carrying a scent that would change the world . . .*

"Pretty cool place to hang out."

Ben had to shake the story out of his head before he could even see who was speaking. Then he had to wonder what the heck Petra Wilde was doing here. She was wearing regular clothes instead of a bathing suit, so maybe she'd gotten tired of hanging out by the pool while everyone else was swimming.

"Mind if I sit down?" Petra said, waving her hand to indicate she meant to sit down on the ground. Ben shrugged. Free country.

"Why have a pool party when it's almost October?"

Petra asked once she'd settled herself on the ground. "Okay, it's still sort of warm outside, but summer's officially over. Why not have a Halloween party?"

Ben didn't reply. He felt strange sitting up high when Petra was down on the ground. He also felt weird because he could see her bra strap at the edge of her shirt's neckband. Were you supposed to say something about that, the way you were when somebody had a piece of spinach stuck in their teeth? His mom said you should, even if it was embarrassing for the person. But no way was he telling Petra anything about her bra. He started tugging at the collar of his own shirt, hoping maybe she'd get the hint.

"I wish we were doing world history instead of ancient history this year, don't you?" Petra asked, scooping up a few pieces of gravel from the dirt. "In world history you get to study China. My dad travels to China a couple of times a year and says it's super interesting."

Well, *that* wasn't the direction Ben had expected this conversation to take. "I read some books about the dynasties last year," he told Petra, happy to finally have something to say. "The Shang and the Zhou and a bunch of others."

"My dad's obsessed with the Yuan," Petra told him. "He's in Beijing a lot on business, and I guess that's where the Yuan were."

"Yeah, that was a pretty good dynasty," Ben said, which was possible the stupidest thing that had ever come out of his mouth. "I mean, because of Kublai Khan and everything. Do you want to sit in my chair?"

Petra smiled at him. "No, thanks. I like it down here. It reminds me of when I was little. My sister and I used to play in the dirt all the time. We made up magic fairylands, stupid stuff like that."

Not stupid at all, Ben wanted to say. He should tell Petra about Willowland, about how on rainy days he and Justin had spent hours at the Yangs' kitchen table, drawing maps and writing descriptions of all the characters and making family trees showing who was related to who and how. Some days Willowland seemed more real to Ben than real life did. It definitely seemed more interesting.

He almost started to say something, but then he

remembered who he was talking to. Petra Wilde was one of *them*. One of the Muggles, as Justin would have put it. She was acting nice enough right now, but if he told her about Willowland, she'd run back to the pool and blab it to everybody. Ben didn't care if they laughed at him about other things—being bad at sports, getting caught with a book in his lap when he was supposed to be listening to the teacher, being friends with Stefan. He didn't care about that.

But if they made fun of Willowland, it would be like a giant coming into the kingdom and crushing it under his foot. Ben would never be able to think about it again, and he liked thinking about Willowland every once in a while. He liked pretending that it was still there, that all he would have to do to bring it back to life was rebuild all those little gravel walls. He'd even written about it in his LA journal, and Mrs. Herrera had left a comment that said, *The pebble in my special collection is from the land of Sylvania, which I discovered in my backyard when I was eight. I plan to return there one day.*

For a teacher, Mrs. Herrera wasn't so bad, Ben

thought now. Maybe he should bring her one of the pieces of Willowland gravel. He wondered if she'd put it in her special collection of special things.

"You don't talk very much, do you?" Petra asked him. "If you talked more, maybe people wouldn't think you were so—well, geeky."

She sounded like one friend giving advice to another. She sounded like she was trying to help him.

Ben wasn't falling for it.

"If I talked more, people would think I was even more geeky," he told her. "Because I am. But I don't really care what people think."

He picked up his book and started reading.

He thought he heard Petra sigh, but he refused to look at her. When he glanced up from his book a minute later, she was walking back across the yard. Only she wasn't walking to the pool; she was headed for the side of the house. There was a good tree for climbing in the side yard, Ben could have told her. A beech tree. He thought about going after her and showing her how to pull herself up into the branches.

But he didn't. He turned the page. *A ball of red flame*

sprang from his hand and flew toward the elf, fast as an arrow . . .

He glanced up one more time, but Petra had disappeared. He hoped she was climbing the tree. He hoped she really didn't think magic worlds were stupid. Because they weren't. At least the real ones weren't.

He'd escaped Lila's party ten minutes early, dropping off *Eragon* in a big box covered in wrapping paper in the foyer. "Sorry you have to leave so soon, Ben!" Lila's mom had called after him.

"I have some friends coming over," he'd lied as he opened the door. "But thanks for inviting me."

She hadn't corrected him, hadn't insisted that Lila had wanted to invite him. She'd just said, "Come over anytime, Ben!"

He waited until he'd pulled the door closed behind him before he started laughing. Come over anytime!

The evening opened up in front of him. Maybe they'd order pizza for dinner, and then Ben and his dad could play a couple of rounds of Star Wars Battlefront, Ben's idea of a perfect night.

He was just about to cross the street when he thought he heard someone call his name. But when he turned around, he didn't see anyone. Still, there it was again: "Goodbye, Ben McPherson!"

It was coming from the beech tree in Justin's—Lila's—side yard.

He'd thought about calling goodbye back, but he didn't.

Thinking about it now, he sort of wished he had.

Chapter Six

petra

Monday, October 2

Sitting in language arts on a Monday morning, Petra Wilde wondered if a person could die of boredom. If so, she was in trouble, because everything in the world bored her. Everything about everyone she knew bored her. She bored herself.

This book they were reading—*Wonder*? Boring. Petra knew how it was going to turn out the minute she started. By the end of the book everyone would love the kid with the strange face. He was smart and funny and kind, and the kids who first didn't want to be his friend because of his face would slowly change their minds as they got to know him. Petra didn't know why she'd bothered finishing the book.

Now if the author had wanted to make the book interesting, she would have made Auggie not that great on the inside. She would have made him really sarcastic, because that was how he protected himself from all the mean things people said. If Petra had had a disability that people made fun of, that was how *she'd* be. She'd make people scared to even look at her.

Of course, a lot of people were already scared to look at Petra—or maybe they looked at her, but they were afraid to talk to her. "You look mean when you're just sitting there," Rosie had told her at the pool one day last summer. "Are you trying to look mean?"

Petra had shrugged. "I'm not trying to do anything. I just look the way I look."

"Well, you're just lucky you're so pretty," Rosie had said quickly, which was typical Rosie. She liked to criticize and then pretend she hadn't. Or dress up her criticism so it seemed like she was worried about you. *Oh, you look so pale today. Are you sick? Or maybe it's the color of your shirt. It sort of washes you out. Are you sure you're not sick?*

Did Ben McPherson think she looked mean? Talking to him at Lila's party Saturday was the closest thing to an interesting conversation Petra had had in ages. He'd looked shocked when she'd started talking about Chinese dynasties, like he couldn't believe someone like her was smart. She wondered what else they might have talked about if he hadn't been his usual Ben McPherson geeky self and clammed up. Petra had all sorts of topics she'd like to discuss. Her mom was currently obsessed with climate change—did Ben think global warming was for real? If he could travel anywhere, where would he go? Petra thought she might like to go to Africa. Ben was half African American; had he ever wanted to go to Africa?

Petra wished for the millionth time that she was in a school where there were at least three people worth talking to. Was that so much to ask for? Last spring she'd applied to the Lakewood Friends School, the only private school her parents could afford, and had been put on a waiting list. Friends School had amazing classes like Spanish Through Spanish-Speaking Artists and Mythic Worlds: Stories and Wisdom from

Past Cultures. If she'd gotten in, Petra had planned on cutting her hair super short and wearing glasses with clear lenses. Her new friends would tell her amazing things that she didn't already know.

Looking around the classroom, Petra wondered if there was one truly interesting person here. Carson Bennett was bent over his spelling workbook, chewing on a pencil. Carson was cute, and he could be funny, but interesting? Doubtful. She wondered if he realized Cammi Lovett was staring at him from across the room, her eyes all dreamy. *He's out of your league, Cammi,* Petra wanted to call over to her, but Cammi, while no Ben McPherson, wasn't stupid. Maybe not interesting, but definitely not dumb. She had to know that a boy like Carson would never go for her.

Rogan was pretty smart and possibly interesting, but you'd probably have to dig pretty deep to get to the interesting parts. Cole Perun didn't do anything but draw all the time, an unusual combo of interesting and totally boring, which wasn't the combination Petra was looking for. That kid Sam, the one who moved a few weeks ago, might have had some hidden depths, now that Petra thought about it. Like new girl Ellie, he was big on taking notes. He seemed like he might have secrets. Secrets could make a person interesting, as long as they weren't the sad sort of secrets that made you want to pretend you'd never heard them.

Speaking of Ellie the new girl, what was her story? And why did Petra still think of Ellie as the new girl, but not Lila, who was new too? But Lila didn't seem new. It was like there had been a spot just waiting for Lila to fill, but the same wasn't true for Ellie. No one had put out a sign saying, WANTED FOR SIXTH GRADE: GIRL WITH FOUNTAIN PEN AND UNCONTROLLABLE CURLY HAIR WHO TRIES TO SNEAK-READ BOOKS IN HER LAP DURING SCIENCE AND MATH PERIODS. Nobody had put in a request for a girl who was either really quiet or sort of braggy about all the places she'd lived.

Ellie Barker was probably an interesting person, Petra had to admit, but she was giving up on geeks after the Ben McPherson fail. So that meant Stefan and Bart were out too. As for Becca Hobbes—Petra looked around the room to see what Becca was doing right this minute. She'd be done with the spelling assignment, which meant she was probably dusting the books in the reading corner or watering Mrs. Herrera's plants on the windowsill next to her desk. Yep, there she was, standing by the teacher's desk, per usual.

But wait a minute. Petra leaned forward, trying to get a better look. Mrs. Herrera was at the Editor's Roundtable with Elizabeth Hernandez, her back to her desk. And Becca seemed to be pouring something from a baggie into Mrs. Herrera's top desk drawer while nervously peeking around to see if anyone was looking. What was she pouring? Sugar? Petra sat back, trying to appear like she wasn't watching. Now Becca slipped something out of her pocket, a little white jewelry box, and opened the lid. She turned the box upside down and tapped on it, like she was trying to get its contents to fall into the drawer. Then she tucked the box back into her pocket and pushed the drawer closed.

"Becca, can I help you with something?" Mrs. Herrera called from the Editor's Roundtable. "What are you looking for?"

"I was checking to see if you had any spelling tests you needed me to grade," Becca replied. Totally unconvincing, in Petra's opinion, but Mrs. Herrera seemed to buy her lame explanation.

"I'll let you know if I need help, thanks," Mrs. Herrera said. "Why don't you find something to read if you're done with your assignment."

"Can I go to the library?" Becca asked. "I finished *Wonder*."

Mrs. Herrera nodded. "Yes, but be back in ten minutes, please."

Petra raised her hand. "Can I go? I'm done too, and I need a new book."

"Of course," Mrs. Herrera said. "Ask Mrs. Rosen for something challenging. I want you to push yourself a little harder, Petra."

That was the interesting thing about Mrs. Herrera—who was possibly the only interesting non-geek person other than Petra in that classroom: she seemed to think Petra was smart. Which Petra was, but she liked to hide it whenever possible.

"I like your shirt," Becca said as they walked out into the hallway. "What would you call that color? Periwinkle?"

"I'd call it blue," Petra informed her. "So what were you putting in Mrs. Herrera's drawer?"

Becca went pale. "Um, what? I wasn't putting anything in her drawer. I was looking for spelling tests to grade. Mrs. Herrera lets me grade our practice tests sometimes."

Petra rolled her eyes. What a simpleton. "We got our practice tests back Friday afternoon, remember? Besides, I saw you pouring something. Was it sugar? And what was in the box?"

Becca's hands started to tremble, and Petra decided to try a different approach. "Come on, Becca, everybody knows you're Mrs. H's favorite. You guys probably play practical jokes on each other all the time. That's what friends do, right? Play practical jokes, have fun?"

To Petra's surprise, Becca's expression turned angry. "I'm definitely not her favorite. I'm more like her unfavorite."

Interesting. So Mrs. Herrera hadn't fallen for Becca's brownnosing routine. Every year Becca Hobbes was held up by teachers as this kind of saint, but any kid—or any adult who couldn't be bought with a

few cookies and a dozen compliments a day—could
see right through her. Petra should have known that
Mrs. Herrera was the sort of teacher who wouldn't be
impressed by Becca's campaign to be teacher's pet.

"Sounds like she did something to make you mad,"
Petra said. "Sounds like maybe you're trying to get back
at her." She moved in closer, put her hand on Becca's
shoulder. "You can tell me. Everyone thinks Mrs.
Herrera is so great, but I guess she's not fooling either
of us."

Becca shook her head. "No way. She's an awful person."

"She really is," Petra said in a soothing voice. "So
what did you do?"

Becca looked to her left and to her right, making
sure no one else was around. She leaned toward Petra
and whispered, "I poured sugar in her drawer, and then
I dumped some ants from our yard in there. I'm hoping
they'll decide her drawer is a great place to live and call
all their friends."

*Or wander around and leave, having no idea where
they are,* Petra thought. What an idiot.

"Don't you think that's a great idea?" Becca giggled, sounding worried at the same time. "Don't you think that will drive her crazy?"

"I think you're brilliant," Petra said. Actually, that was the opposite of what she thought, but who cared? Because even if Becca was incredibly dumb for someone who got straight As, and even if she wasn't interesting as a person, she might possibly be interesting as a project. Could Petra transform Miss Goody Two-shoes of the sixth grade into an eleven-year-old juvenile delinquent? Yes, Petra thought. She believed she could. Maybe she could convince Becca to steal one of Mrs. Herrera's special things from her special collection. If Becca was so down on their teacher, it might be easy to convince her the best revenge would be to nab those fancy little sugar cubes. Talk about your ant bait!

"You don't want to eat lunch with me tomorrow, do you?" Petra said. "Because I'd really like to get your advice on something."

Becca's eyes widened until Petra thought they were going to pop out of her head. "I'd—I'd love to."

"Great," Petra said. "Now I guess we better go check out some books—unless you want to do something else instead?"

They were standing outside the art room. The door was wide open, but the room was empty, and Petra made a quick inventory of ways to send Becca over to the dark side. Splash paint on the artwork hanging on the walls? Write mean things on the whiteboard about Mrs. Lamprey, the art teacher? Take Mrs. Lamprey's scissors—the fancy ones that only the teacher was allowed to use—and cut up . . . what? What could they cut up?

Petra looked at Becca, who was staring at her wide-eyed, her expression full of expectation. Becca's hair—which was pretty, Petra had to admit—was pulled back in a long ponytail.

"You've got great hair," she said, and Becca's cheeks flushed red. "Have you ever thought about cutting it? I could definitely see you with a shorter cut. Something kind of punky and rebellious."

Becca looked uncertain, but Petra took her by the hand and pulled her into the art room. "You need to show people you're not the Becca Hobbes you used to be. You don't care what other people think! Especially not Mrs. Herrera. She needs to know she's dealing with a new you."

The scissors were on Mrs. Lamprey's desk, the sharp blades gleaming. Petra smiled. Oh, this was going to be an interesting project, all right. As interesting as she could possibly make it.

Chapter Seven

Ellie

Monday, October 2

Some writers took notes on their characters and made outlines of their stories before they started writing their novels, and others jumped in with only the slightest idea of what their story might be about. Ellie knew that J. K. Rowling was in the first group of writers, and so she decided that was the kind of writer she would be too. A planner and a plotter.

She'd spent the weekend taking notes on all the kids in her class. Well, not on all of them. She knew absolutely nothing about Ethan Lantzy, for instance, other than that he was obsessed with lacrosse, and Felicity

Wallack was a mystery to her. All Ellie knew about Felicity was that her two best friends were in Mr. Lee's class, and so in a way it seemed like Felicity was in Mr. Lee's class too, because at recess and lunch and PE that was where you'd find her, over with Lee's Bees, tucked between Madeline Connor and Anna Ross.

Ellie liked making lists, so that was the first thing she did: make a list of where everyone seemed to fit in. Her categories included Popular Boys, Popular Girls, Friendly and Nice Boys, Friendly and Nice Girls, Athletes, Shy People, Book People, People with Special Talents and Skills, and Uncategorizable People. She'd thought about making a category for People who Bring Good Lunches, and People Who Wear Cool Shoes, but then she decided she was overdoing it. It would probably be better to do an entry for each person in which she described their lunches and clothes and the kind of jokes they liked to make and who their friends were. Yes, that was exactly what she'd do. But first she would do categories.

Popular Boys was easy: Carson Bennett (cute, but goofy), Garrison Paul (stuck-up and full of himself), and Matt Collins (bully). Popular Girls, also easy: Petra Wilde, Rosie Nichols, and Lila Willis (meanest, almost as mean, jerk).

Friendly and Nice Boys: Rogan Kimari, Henry Lloyd (sort of—maybe not really? He could be a big pest, but he wasn't mean), and Cole Perun. Ethan Lantzy seemed nice—Ellie would pencil him in, she decided, and then observe and take notes over several days in order to confirm. Stefan Morrisey also seemed nice, but he was too quiet to be called friendly.

Friendly and Nice Girls: Cammi Lovett, Ariana Savarino, Elizabeth Hernandez. Aadita Amrit was clearly nice and might be friendly, but like Stefan she was very quiet. Still, Ella put her in the Friendly and Nice group, because Aadita had friendliness potential. Of course, if she was going to do that for Aadita, she ought to do it for Stefan, too. She went ahead and penciled him in under Ethan.

The longer she worked on her lists, the more she realized she didn't know enough about her classmates to write a novel about them. All she knew about Carson Bennett, for instance, was that he was popular, a vegetarian, and made lots of dumb jokes that everyone laughed at because he was popular and that was one of the perks of being popular—people laughed at your jokes even if the jokes were dumb. Did he play sports? It seemed like he should play sports, but he never wore a jersey on soccer game day. What was up with that? Maybe he was on a travel team. Maybe he was too good for middle school soccer. How could Ellie find out?

There was no getting around it: she was going to have to do research. The good news was that she loved doing research. Also, she loved spying on people and eavesdropping on their conversations.

So on Monday Ellie went to school with a new notebook and a new plan. Every day she was going to focus on three people, observe their habits, note who they ate lunch with, and generally look for clues and insights about what they liked and disliked. She'd describe what they were wearing and also their fingernails. Ellie thought fingernails said a lot about a person. Clean, dirty, bitten, clipped, polished, these fingernail conditions were like little signs people waved all day long, signs that said I'M NEAT! Or I'M

NERVOUS! Or I DIDN'T TAKE A SHOWER THIS MORNING!

It only took Ellie a little while to figure out that you could observe people during class time, but it was hard to observe them doing anything interesting. Stefan Morrisey was on her Monday list, but all he did during first period was raise his hand a lot and get a disappointed look on his face when their science teacher, Mrs. Kafsky, said, "Does anyone besides Stefan have the answer to that question? I know Stefan is not the only one in this room who did the homework assignment." When Mrs. Kafsky gave them the last ten minutes to get started on their homework, Stefan finished his in five and then spent the rest of the time reading a book whose title Ellie couldn't make out.

She got as close as she could to Ethan, her second victim, as the class went to Mrs. Hulka's room for history, but he didn't do anything notable in the forty-five seconds it took to get from one room to the other except to turn to Henry Lloyd and say, "History sucks, dude."

By LA, back in Mrs. Herrera's classroom, Ellie was starting to think that school might be the worst place to observe people, especially someone like Aadita (the third person on Monday's list), who very rarely said or did anything. How could anyone be so utterly, fantastically quiet? Sometimes Ellie wanted to yell at the top of her lungs just to erase some of the silence that Aadita created.

Maybe school just wasn't a place where people could be interesting, Ellie thought as the clock ticked away the last few minutes of the period. Maybe it squashed the interesting right out of people.

Two seconds later a sharp knock on the door caused Ellie and everybody else to look up at the same time. Henry Lloyd dropped his pencil and yelled, "Whoops!" and Mrs. Herrera issued a sharp, "Quiet, Henry!" Then she looked around the classroom and said, "Cammi, would you open—"

But there wasn't time for Cammi to open the door. The vice principal, Mrs. Whalen, stormed into the classroom before Cammi could manage to get out of her seat.

"I need to speak to you in the hallway, Mrs. Herrera," she announced. "We've got art room shenanigans on our hands."

Art room shenanigans, Ellie happily wrote in her notebook.

"Would you mind telling me—"

Again, Mrs. Herrera was cut off midsentence.

"Outside, Mrs. Herrera," the vice principal ordered, as she marched back out of the room, calling, "Becca Hobbes, I told you not to move a muscle!"

Becca Hobbes got caught doing something bad? Immediately the class hummed with doubt, and Ellie took notes as fast as she could. Some of the kids had known Becca since preschool, and she'd never gotten in trouble for so much as whispering when she was supposed to be working on an assignment. She'd never talked in the hall or stuck chewing gum under her desk or dog-eared a library book to mark her place. Late homework? Never. Cut in front of somebody in line? Nope, not the type.

"Quiet down," Mrs. Herrera said when their whispers grew to a near roar. "I'm going to go speak with Mrs. Whalen. Ben is in charge until I return."

Ben looked up from his book, glanced around the classroom, and then returned to his reading. It was

Rogan Kimari who walked to the front of the class-room, put a finger to his lips, and then went to stand by the pencil sharpener next to the door.

"What's going on?" Ethan called in a loud whisper, and everyone went, "Shhh!" at the same time.

Rogan practically had his ear against the door, his face turned toward the class. At one point, his eyes got really wide, and Ethan said, "What?" and everyone shushed him again.

"Quick, somebody throw me a pencil!" Rogan whisper-yelled a few seconds later, and Matt threw a pencil so hard that you could hear a little thud when it hit Rogan in the head. Ellie admired how cool Rogan was about it, picking up the pencil from the floor, calmly inserting it into the sharpener, and acting like he didn't even notice when someone pushed open the door. But as soon as he saw Petra, he took a step back and yelled, "Whoa! What happened to your hair?"

Petra ignored him, and so did Becca as she followed Petra inside. Ellie sat back in her chair—hard. What the heck had happened to those two on the way to the library? Had they been kidnapped by an insane barber? It was hard to say which girl looked less like herself. They both had shaggy pixie cuts now, but on Becca it looked sort of glamorous, like a French movie star. Petra, on the other hand, resembled a dandelion with its seeds blown off. Studying Petra, Ellie suddenly understood why every other TV commercial was for hair products. Hair, it turned out, was powerful.

Petra looked like a girl who'd lost her power.

"Petra, what did you do?" Rosie gasped, sounding horrified. "Your hair is ridiculous!"

Mrs. Whalen stood in the doorway. "Mrs. Lamprey nearly had a heart attack when she walked into her classroom and saw these two, and I don't blame her." She looked sternly at the class. "You're not in elementary school anymore. You're expected to act like young adults in middle school. You don't skip class to give each other haircuts. You don't cut off all your hair and get it in the paint! Mrs. Lamprey spent all morning mixing that paint!"

A bunch of kids laughed, but not Ellie. This was just too strange. Becca Hobbes wasn't supposed to look like a French movie star. Petra Wilde wasn't supposed to look like a wilted petunia. Ellie felt like she was watching a show on the Disney Channel, where two kids switch bodies. Not that Becca used to look like a wilted petunia before . . . Ellie sighed. She couldn't explain the weirdness. She just knew that the scene in front of her was very, very strange.

Mrs. Whalen turned toward the hallway and motioned Mrs. Herrera into the classroom. Everyone was silent when Mrs. Herrera walked back inside, and because the room was silent, everyone heard Mrs. Whalen whisper, "We are getting very, very close to having a problem here, Judith. After what happened last year, the words 'thin ice' come to mind."

Who was on thin ice? Ellie wondered, and looking around at her classmates, she could tell they were wondering the same thing. It had to be Mrs. Herrera, right? Petra and Becca hadn't been at this school last year, and if Becca was in trouble, this was the first time ever. Usually you had to get in trouble three or four times before you were in thin-ice territory.

Ellie wished she had friends to discuss this with. There was so much to talk about! So much to dissect.

You had the Petra-Becca situation, and the Mrs.-Herrera-on-thin-ice situation, and Ellie thought the two situations were probably connected, but it was the sort of thing you needed to work through with at least one other person, preferably a small group of people. She wanted to know what Rogan had overheard. Did anyone have any idea of what had happened in Mrs. Herrera's class last year? Had there been a series of art room shenanigans? Were art room shenanigans a thing with Mrs. Herrera's students?

As soon as the bell rang at the end of the day, everyone shot out of the building, probably so they could get on their buses as fast as possible and start texting each other about the day's events. But Ellie didn't have anyone to text. All she could do was get on her bus and think.

She wished that bus rides weren't too bumpy for taking notes, because she had ten million thoughts and impressions rushing around her brain and she wanted to get all of them down on paper. How to describe the way she felt when she saw Petra Wilde looking like the opposite of Petra Wilde? How to describe the mean smile that played around Becca's lips when Mrs. Herrera said, "Don't worry, Becca. Your hair will grow back faster than you think." The old Becca would have said, *Oh, thank you, Mrs. Herrera! I feel so much better, Mrs. Herrera!* This new Becca didn't seem like she cared all that much about Mrs. Herrera's opinion.

Ellie stared out the window at all the kids streaming to their buses. They looked so normal. Ellie was starting to wonder whether you could really tell if someone was normal by how they seemed on the outside. Petra Wilde had always looked normal—better than normal, really. She looked perfect. But this afternoon? Not so much. She was like that kid outside the bus window just now, the one who was working his way against the current of students leaving for the day. Maybe he had a reason for going in the wrong direction, but it still seemed strange.

It took Ellie a second to realize the kid was Sam Hawkins, the boy whose family had moved a couple of weeks ago—or "relocated," as Mrs. Herrera had put it. What was he doing here? Had his family moved back?

Seeing Sam just added to Ellie's feeling that something was off about today.

Ellie wondered what Cammi had been thinking when she saw Becca with her new hairdo. What would it be like to see your best friend completely transformed? Would Becca's hair change their friendship?

It would be so nice to have a best friend to discuss this with, Ellie thought as the bus pulled away from the school. Of course all she wanted at this point was any kind of friend. She'd like to have someone to sit with at lunch and talk about the things that she found interesting. She'd like to talk about the Weasleys, Ellie's favorite fictional family. Sometimes she pretended she *was* a Weasley—that she and Ginny Weasley were twins and Ron was her overprotective big brother. She'd even written some stories about her life as a Weasley, and it would be nice to have a friend to share these stories with.

They'd almost reached her neighborhood when a girl in an oversize hoodie plopped down beside Ellie. Ellie recognized her as one of the kids who got on the bus in the morning two stops after hers.

"So what's the deal with the haircut situation?" the girl asked. "All of a sudden, Petra looks like a drowned rat."

"How did you hear about that?" Ellie asked, at the same time wondering how this girl would know that she might have some inside information.

"I'm friends with Felicity, and she texted me a few minutes ago. I know you're in Mrs. Herrera's class, so I thought I'd ask."

How do you know? Ellie wanted to ask. *Someone actually knows about me? My presence has been noted?*

"I'm Charlotte, by the way," the girl said, sticking out her hand.

Ellie shook it. "Ellie. I'm new this year."

"I figured," Charlotte said. "Otherwise, we would have been on the same bus last year. So being new, do you understand the absolute weirdness of Becca Hobbes doing something like that—something that might actually get her in trouble, even if it was just messing up the art room?"

Ellie reached into her backpack, pulled out her notebook, and began to read the notes she'd jotted down in

LA. "In recollections of Becca dating back to the two-day twos preschool class, there is not one memory of her committing even the most minor of offenses. Cammi Lovett seems to recall that once in kindergarten Becca dripped three beads of glue on her desk to make a glue-bead necklace, but the guilt proved too much and she washed them off before they had time to dry."

"That is the essence of Becca Hobbes," Charlotte said. "What's got everyone in a tizzy is the fact that not only did Becca cut off all her hair, but she did it in cahoots with Petra Wilde. It's sort of like the pope and a serial killer hanging out together. A conundrum."

"It's a mystery, all right," Ellie admitted. "I wonder if Petra was trying to get Becca in trouble as a joke."

"But why did she cut her hair too? I hear that Rosie has already posted Petra's picture all over the Internet—name your platform, and you'll find her very unbecoming new look."

"I thought Rosie was Petra's best friend," Ellie said. "Why would she do that?"

Charlotte raised an eyebrow. "Rosie is nobody's friend."

"Not even her best friend's friend," Ellie mused. "That's pretty sad."

The bus pulled to the curb and the doors squealed open. "Well, this is me," Charlotte said as she stood up. "Thanks for the info."

"Gingie, wait up!" someone called from the back of the bus. "Help me carry my project."

"Siblings," Charlotte said with a sigh. "Older siblings are the worst."

"'Gingie'?" Ellie asked.

"Family nickname. We've all got them. You should—"

Before Charlotte could finish, a tall girl with red hair pulled back into a braid dumped a bulging canvas tote bag into her arms. "Do not drop this, do you hear me?"

"Yes, Your Highness," Charlotte replied, sinking a little under the bag's weight.

What should I do? Ellie wanted to call after her. *I'll do anything! Let's be friends!*

"See you tomorrow!" Charlotte yelled over her shoulder.

"Okay, that would be great!" Ellie called back, realizing as soon as the words were out of her mouth how stupid they sounded. She leaned back against the seat and sighed. She'd been *this* close to making a friend and somehow she'd blown it. It was like she didn't know how to close the deal anymore. *Oh well,* she thought as she sat back up and pulled a pen out of her backpack, *at least I have my notebook.* That could be the title of her next book: *My Notebook, My Bestie.* And even though the road was bumpy and the bus shimmied and jerked, Ellie did what she always did in times of trouble. She wrote.

Chapter Eight

Rogan

Tuesday, October 3

Rogan Kimari and his friends weren't into drama. When they got together after school or on weekends to play basketball or Assassin's Creed, they didn't talk about who liked who, or who was mad at who, or who wore what. Rogan had two older sisters, so he knew that girls talked about all that stuff, and his sisters swore that boys did too, but not the boys Rogan was friends with. They talked sports, they talked gaming, and sometimes they compared notes about teachers and homework. But girl stuff? No. Because they weren't girls.

But when Petra Wilde walked into science on Tuesday, Rogan had to admit he wouldn't mind talking to somebody about the thing with Petra and Becca cutting their hair off. Because while he thought he pretty much got girls (when you had two older sisters, you could write a book), he didn't get *that*. It didn't make sense, and Rogan liked things to make sense.

It was like basic science, right? You had Petra, who was a creep, but she was a popular creep and kept her distance from mere mortals. Becca Hobbes, definitely a mere mortal, was also a butt kisser who tried to get in good with every adult on the planet. Add Becca to Petra and you got—nothing. They were repelling magnets. No matter how hard you squeezed them together, there was always going to be a force field that kept them apart.

Until yesterday. Man, that had been bizarre when they'd walked into the classroom. Rogan had heard the whole conversation in the hallway—*Mrs. Lamprey caught these girls in the art room, blah blah blah, they said they couldn't explain why they did it, blah blah blah, you need to keep your class under better control, blah blah blah.* None of it had prepared Rogan for what Becca and Petra looked like when they'd walked back into the classroom.

Becca looked like someone had vacuumed all the goody-goody right out of her. She looked like this girl named Gretchen his sisters were sort of friends with. Gretchen skipped classes and stayed out late on Saturdays and had a boyfriend who'd dropped out of high school. Rogan's mom didn't like Gretchen because she thought Gretchen was a bad influence.

Becca Hobbes looked like a bad influence.

Petra just looked weird. Rogan had never thought she was all that pretty to begin with, the way everybody else did, but now her eyes looked humongous and her head looked too big for the rest of her body. She looked like an idiot, really. It was a total mystery why she'd cut her hair off like that. Rogan definitely didn't get it.

Why Mrs. Herrera was on thin ice was another mystery. Ethan's mom was vice president of the PTA, and he was going to see if he could find anything out, like if Mrs. Herrera had a criminal record or if some of her students last year had also gotten in trouble in the art room. She didn't seem like the kind of teacher who let her students go wild, though. In fact, she had the most rules about classroom behavior of any of the sixth-grade teachers.

"You'll be pleased to hear that we're spending the class period outdoors," Mrs. Kafsky, their science teacher, announced as she walked around the room to collect last night's homework. "That's right, it's outdoor journal day!"

"Can I bring my dog?" Henry asked, and half the class laughed and the other half shushed him. Rogan thought they should have a Henry journal day, where they all made observations about Henry and tried to figure out what was wrong with him.

"Not today, Henry," Mrs. Kafsky said. "Just your note-book and your partner. That reminds me—everybody grab a partner!"

Rogan twisted around in his seat to see if Cole or Ethan wanted to be partners, but they were sitting next to each other and had already partnered up. Okay, so who else might be good? He was about to call across the classroom to Stefan (something you could do in

Mrs. Kafsky's class, but not in Mrs. Herrera's) when Petra punched him lightly on the shoulder.

"Would you mind being my partner?" she asked. "I hate to ask, but . . ."

That *but* hung out there between them, and Rogan wondered how Petra would finish her sentence. *But as a result of recent events, I have zero friends? But if you don't partner with me, nobody will? But I'm madly in love with you and this is the chance I've been waiting for all my life?*

"Uh, uh, sure," Rogan stammered when Petra didn't bother to finish her sentence, wishing he had the guts to say, *Are you kidding? Are you mentally insane?* "I mean, you're good at science, right?"

"I'm a genius," Petra said. "I'm Einstein. I'm Madame Curie."

"Um, okay," Rogan said. "Whatever."

Her hair was kind of sticking up today, like she'd put some kind of goop in it. He hoped everybody started calling her Goopy Girl.

The way everyone called him Booger Boy.

Not a day had gone by that someone didn't pass

Rogan in the hall or stop by his desk and say, "Hey, Booger Boy, let's do a finger check!" Or "Hey, Booger Boy, find any good ones today?" And it was all Petra Wilde's fault. She was the one who'd walked by his desk in math the second week of school and said in a loud voice, "Kind of gross, that booger-picking thing you do," like she'd caught Rogan with his finger up his nose. "Maybe it's time to grow up and use a Kleenex, Booger Boy."

Rogan, who would admit to picking his nose in the privacy of his room, had not been picking his nose, and it didn't occur to him right away that Petra was saying *he* was the Booger Boy. He'd been thinking about the postcard written in Chinese that Mrs. Herrera had in her special collection of special things, and whether or not he should take Chinese next year like his dad wanted him to. He'd been thinking about how hard it would be to learn the Chinese alphabet, and how he'd rather focus on getting better at lacrosse so he could be a starter next season.

The one thing he hadn't been doing was picking his nose. He never picked his nose at school. His sisters had pounded that into his head: no public nose picking!

He'd looked up at the sound of Petra's voice, not sure who she'd been talking to, but already feeling sorry for whoever it was, because once Petra decided you were one thing or another, it stuck.

How many seconds did it take for Rogan to realize that Petra was talking to him? How long before he felt this hollow, icy feeling in his stomach, followed by the thought that he sort of wanted to throw up? How long before he heard everyone around him laughing? How long before he realized he was going to have to work really, really hard not to cry?

Pretending to ignore Petra, he'd looked back down at his math book. His heart was racing, like Ethan or Cole had just jumped out from behind a door. Ethan and Cole and Rogan were always pulling stupid pranks to scare each other and they were always calling each other names and making jokes—but they were friends. That was what friends did. Friends farted and blamed it on somebody else. Friends ragged on each other for having butt-faces. It was funny. It was—well, friendly.

Petra wasn't being friendly. She was being mean, and Rogan wasn't used to people being mean to him. His sisters teased him, but most of the time they treated him like he was their mascot or something. It drove Rogan crazy, actually, but as he sat there with his face practically on his desk, he missed his sisters. He wished they'd walk into the room and grab him and take him home. He wished his mom would magically appear and offer to make him a grilled cheese sandwich.

Thinking about his mom had been a mistake. It was like a signal to start crying. Rogan did his best to resist, but a few of the tears dripped out onto the page of his book. Rogan swallowed. He tried to toughen up, to think about his dad, think about playing Madden Football with him on Saturday afternoons. That was kind of their thing. *Guy Time*, his dad called it. Sometimes they made nachos for Guy Time, even though the controls got all greasy from their cheesy fingers. His dad would have helped Rogan come up with a sarcastic comeback, something that would have made Petra turn red and scurry back to her seat. Then Rogan and his dad would have slapped high fives. They would have laughed so hard one of them would have farted.

Ethan and Cole had waited by his desk at the end of class while he put his stuff in his backpack. They didn't say anything about Petra or boogers. They talked about lacrosse instead, and what a dud goalie Luke was and how they were dead if the team was stuck with him all season. Rogan talked about Luke too, but the whole time his brain was scrambling for a comeback. *Funny you should say that, Petra, because, because, because—* but he couldn't think of one thing. He tried to come up with something for weeks, but he never did.

So maybe he didn't understand the whole haircut fiasco, but when Petra Wilde had walked back into LA looking like a nearly bald lemur, it had been one of the happiest moments of Rogan's life.

Now, as the class walked out the back exit and onto the playground, he glanced at his notebook to reread Mrs. Kafsky's assignment. "Note the effects of recent weather systems on the environment." Normally he was pretty good at science, but for some reason this assignment seemed to be written in another language.

His brain was all confused, probably from having to partner with Petra's brain.

"I wonder what she means by recent weather systems?" Petra asked, walking up behind Rogan. "I mean, recent as in yesterday, or recent in the last six months? Because if it's the last six months, you can tell that the trees by the fence got pretty damaged by some of the storms this summer. You want to go look?"

Rogan nodded mutely and followed Petra as she walked toward the fence at the edge of the blacktop.

"See that, up in that oak tree?" Petra pointed toward some half-attached branches in a tree that looked tired, like it had lost a fight.

"How do you know it's an oak?" Rogan's voice sounded squeaky in his ears, like he was a little mouse. He wanted to kick himself, but instead he squinted upward. *Be cool,* he told himself. *Just shut up and be cool.*

"My mom has an app that identifies trees and plants. You take a picture and the app tells you what it is. Besides, mostly it's oaks around here. My aunt and uncle live in the eastern part of the state where it's all pines, and everything looks so different. Like another planet. Anyway, we better write this stuff down."

Was it an act, Petra talking like she was a normal human being? Had little pieces of hair gotten into her brain? Probably, Rogan thought as he wrote down his observations. Then he looked around the playing fields because he couldn't let Goopy Girl make all their scientific discoveries. "Over there," he said, nodding toward the baseball field, where the earth sloped into a gentle hill behind the home team dugout. "There was a lot of rain last week, so maybe it's swampy at the bottom of that hill. And if it is, maybe we'll find frogs."

"I love frogs," Petra said, sounding perfectly serious. "My mom has an app for frogs, too."

Rogan thought he'd like to meet Petra's mom. She sounded like an interesting person. He wondered if she knew what a jerk her daughter was.

They reached the hill behind the dugout, and sure enough, there was a long, thin puddle at its base. "Look!" Rogan said in a loud whisper, forgetting to be cool. "A bird!"

"My mom doesn't have a bird app," Petra whispered back. "What do you think it is? A sparrow?"

"It's usually a sparrow," Rogan said. "Or a wren."

"Let's put sparrow."

They each wrote in their notebooks. Rogan would have liked to have written something about Petra while he was at it, how she was smarter than he'd thought she was and how this fake nice act was getting on his nerves. Of course she was acting nice. She'd totally messed up yesterday, so now she had to act like a real human being so everyone would like her again. Not that everyone liked her before. Actually, nobody liked her before. But she'd been this kind of queen and people had been scared of her. Now they were freaked out by her, the way her head looked so big and her hair stuck out in little tufts, and that was a totally different thing. Petra would probably do anything to get back on her throne. Even act like she was a decent human being.

Okay, well, if she was so nice now, maybe it was time for Rogan to get to the bottom of what had been bugging him ever since the first week of September.

"So that thing about me picking my nose when I wasn't actually picking my nose?" he said as they started walking back to the school building. He could hear how dumb he sounded, but he had to ask. "Why say it? Why say it to me? Because I wasn't. Picking my nose, I mean. I was just sitting there doing my math."

"What?" Petra stopped walking and turned to look at him. "I have no idea what you're talking about."

"That time in math you told me to quit picking my nose and I wasn't picking my nose?" Rogan repeated. "Why did you do that?"

Petra shrugged. "I really don't remember."

Rogan could feel his face grow hot. "So you're saying you never said it?"

"No," Petra said. "I'm saying I don't remember saying it. I probably did say it, though. It's kind of what I'm good at."

"Everybody calls me 'Booger Boy' now, so thanks for that," Rogan told her. He turned and started walking again. "It's really what I hoped would happen this year."

Petra trailed behind him for a few feet before saying anything. When she caught up, she touched Rogan on the shoulder. "I've decided I'm not going to say stuff like that anymore."

Like Rogan cared. But he couldn't help but asking, "Why not? Because of your hair?"

"My hair? What's wrong with my hair?" Petra asked, and then she laughed, like what had happened to her hair was some kind of private joke. "No, it's not because of my hair. It's just because . . . I guess it's just boring to say that kind of stuff. There are a lot more interesting things to talk about, right?"

Rogan stared at her. "Do you get that I was not picking my nose? Because I can't tell if you understand that you totally made that up."

"I get it," Petra said. "And I'm sorry. I would be happy to issue a statement that I have never seen you picking your nose and that I'm pretty sure you have never produced a booger in your life."

"Yeah, whatever," Rogan said. "Well, anyway, sorry about your hair. Maybe it'll grow back one day."

To his surprise, Petra looked—what? Embarrassed? Hurt? Whatever she was feeling, she just shrugged and started walking in the other direction. "Okay," she said, "thanks, whatever," and Rogan waited for her to add "Booger Boy," but she didn't.

Mrs. Kafsky whistled and yelled, "All right, scientists, let's head back to the classroom and report our findings!"

Rogan found Ethan and Cole over near the jungle gym. "Make any great discoveries?" he asked them as they followed Mrs. Kafsky inside, and when they shook their heads no, he said, "I found a sparrow in a puddle. Pretty big deal."

"How was the hairless wonder?" Ethan asked. "Did she ask you if she could shave your head?"

"She was goopy," Rogan said. "Totally Goopy Girl."

He really didn't want to talk about Petra. He didn't want to think about her, or her hair, or the fact that the last thing he'd said to her was sort of mean, but it didn't feel good to say it, not the way he thought it would.

Scientifically speaking, it had felt pretty bad.

Chapter Nine

Ariana

Wednesday, October 4

ALL Wednesday morning Ariana couldn't stop glancing over at her lunch bag, which was hanging from a peg in her cubby. She could hardly concentrate, she felt so excited about the invitations stowed beneath her sandwich and chips. She was going to have a party, and she loved throwing parties!

Okay, not really a party. For a party you needed at least six people. Not that that was a rule, but it was one of Ariana's Guidelines for a Happy Life. With six people, you could have two teams of three for games, which made it so much more exciting than two teams of two. But Ariana's mom said she could only invite three girls for Saturday, so really it wasn't a party, it was just a plain old sleepover.

But sleepovers were good! Sleepovers meant popcorn and movies and séances and ghost stories. She'd had a sleepover in August with Meryl and Katie and Schuyler from Girl Scouts, and they'd acted out scenes from *Little House on the Prairie*, even though they admitted to each other they were probably too old for that kind of pretend play. Still, they'd had so much fun! Ariana played Nellie Oleson, which was especially neat because she got to be mean and cranky, which was totally the opposite of who Ariana was. Her mom always said she was born with the cheerful gene, which was a good thing, right? Better to be cheerful than to be like Lila or Rosie, always sneering and scowling and looking down their noses at people.

Finally the clock read 11:40—time for lunch! Okay, 11:40 was actually a little early for lunch, but Ariana had started to think of it as *elevenses* instead of lunchtime, ever since her mom packed a note in her lunch that read, *"Nearly eleven o'clock," said Pooh happily.*

"You're just in time for a little smackerel of something." Ariana knew she was too old for Pooh the same way she was too old for *Little House* or Barbies, but Pooh made her so happy! Why shouldn't she be happy?

She'd stored the invitations in her lunch bag because she planned on handing them out at lunch: one for Ellie Barker, one for Becca Hobbes, and one for Elizabeth Hernandez. Although she wasn't advertising it, this was really a Get Well Soon, Becca! party. Because something was clearly wrong with Becca Hobbes. First there was the whole haircutting incident on Monday, which you had to admit was pretty strange, even if it probably was all Petra Wilde's fault. But then yesterday Ariana had seen Becca dog-earing books in the book nook! Mrs. Herrera made a big deal about treating books like sacred objects and set out baskets of bookmarks all over her classroom so that no one would ever feel like they didn't have a choice but to mark their place by bending over the corner of the page.

It felt crazy to Ariana, seeing Becca dog-ear those books! What was next? Was she going to rob the school store? Spray-paint graffiti all over the playground?

Becca clearly needed her help, and a sleepover was a great place to start. In fact, Ariana was almost glad it wasn't going to be a regular sort of party. A sleepover would be small and intimate. And Ellie and Elizabeth were the perfect people to invite. Ellie because she was new and didn't have the same expectations of Becca's behavior that everyone else did, and Elizabeth because she was so nice.

When she got to the cafeteria, she found Elizabeth sitting with Aadita and Cammi. For some reason, Ariana had pictured Elizabeth, Becca, and Ellie sitting together, which of course they never did, but it would have made handing out invitations a lot more convenient. Now she'd have to wait until they went out on the playground after lunch. She certainly couldn't give Elizabeth an invitation and not give Aadita and Cammi one. Gosh, it was strange to see Cammi without Becca by her side! It was like Pooh without Piglet, Calvin without Hobbes, Curious George without the Man in the Yellow Hat.

When Cammi saw her, she clamped her mouth shut, and Ariana wondered what they'd been talking about.

Her? That seemed pretty unlikely. What could you say about Ariana Savarino behind her back that you wouldn't be perfectly happy to say to her face?

"What?" she said as she sat down next to Elizabeth. "What were you guys talking about?"

As usual, Aadita smiled shyly but didn't speak. Cammi shrugged and took a bite of her sandwich. Finally Elizabeth said, "Well, it wasn't gossiping, but we were talking about Petra. Do you know what Henry just told us?"

"That Petra is a space alien?" Ariana said, and laughed at her own joke. That was exactly the sort of thing Henry would say.

"No! Not even close!" Elizabeth said, and then she started giggling so hard she couldn't finish.

"Tell me!" Ariana said. "I mean, it's not something horrible, right?"

"He said that Petra's in love with him and is going to ask him to the Fall Ball," Cammi said, shaking her head at how ridiculous that was. "That's why she cut her hair, so that only someone like Henry would see her beauty. Classic Henry! But seriously, do you think something terrible happened to Petra? I mean, like, are her parents getting a divorce? Because otherwise, what would explain how weird she's gotten?"

"How do you explain how weird *Becca's* gotten?" Elizabeth asked Cammi. "I mean not to judge or be rude? But it's like Becca's become a completely different person in just a few days. What has she said to you about what happened on Monday?"

Cammi shrugged. "She won't talk to me. Not on the bus, not at school. She won't answer my texts, either. Partly I think she's mad because Carson's her crush, and he and I are sort of study buddies now. Strictly as friends, though."

Like there was a possibility of Carson liking Cammi as more than a friend! Ariana had to stop herself from rolling her eyes. "Did Becca know that on Monday? Because maybe that's why she cut her hair—to make herself look pretty."

Which definitely didn't work, Ariana thought (but would of course never say out loud).

"I don't think so," Cammi said. "I didn't mention that Carson and I were studying together. The thing is, I feel really bad, but at the same time, Becca and I have sort of been growing apart."

Ariana gave Cammi a sympathetic smile. Sort of a convenient time to grow apart, she thought, but whatever.

"Anyway," Cammi continued, "Carson says he never understood how Becca and I were friends in the first place, we're so different. I told him it's mostly because we live on the same street. It's like we were automatically friends because we were the same age." She paused and then said, "Why are you giving me that look, Ariana? I'm just saying the truth."

What look? Ariana wasn't giving anyone a look. "Sorry, I just remembered something my mom asked me to do that I totally forgot about."

"Yeah, right," Cammi said before biting into an apple.

"When did you and Carson get to be such good friends?" Elizabeth asked. "Do you like him? I mean, *like him* like him?"

"We're just friends who study together," Cammi repeated, sounding like it was no big deal, even though clearly it was. "We have the same sense of humor."

Uh-huh. Ariana took out her sandwich and examined it, trying not to make eye contact with anyone. Turkey and avocado, mustard, cut into four neat squares, no crust, no mayo, just the way she liked it. "So I thought I saw Sam yesterday afternoon," she announced, deciding it was time for a new subject. "In the hallway after the last bell."

"Sam who used to be in our class?" Elizabeth asked. "Why would he be back at school? I thought he moved."

"Maybe he's moving back," Ariana said. "Maybe he missed us so much he couldn't stay away!"

Ariana liked that idea. Not that she'd liked Sam, but he was kind of cute, and it was fun to think that maybe he'd fallen for someone (not her, of course!) and had come back to catch a glimpse of his true love from time to time.

"Carson said he saw him too," Cammi said. "On Monday, I think. He must not have moved too far if he's coming back all the time."

Elizabeth nodded. "A lot of my swim team friends live pretty close to here, but they go to New Hope Middle. Maybe that's where Sam goes now."

Ariana looked around the cafeteria as though she might find Sam there now (not that she cared if he was or not). People were beginning to pack up their lunches and head for the places they usually headed for. Ben, Stefan, and Bart would spend the rest of the period in the computer lab, and Ethan, Cole, and Rogan (Booger Boy!) were collecting their lacrosse sticks so they could get in some playground practice. Rosie and Lila had their heads close together, probably talking about bizarro Petra (they wouldn't bother discussing bizarro Becca; Becca was too far below them). When they left the cafeteria, they'd go over to the picnic table where the popular girls from the different homerooms gathered and plotted how to make other people miserable.

Where was Petra? Well, wherever she was, Ariana hoped she was okay. Really! Just because Petra had told her in fifth grade that she looked like a rabbit—"Your nose is always twitching; are you aware of that?" Petra had asked in the middle of reading group—didn't mean Ariana hated her. She didn't hate anyone!

Glancing up at the clock—11:35, recess time—

Ariana realized she'd barely touched her sandwich. But that was okay. She was too excited to eat—she was throwing a party! No, not a party—a sleepover. She laughed to herself. How could she keep forgetting it was a sleepover? She guessed it just felt like a party to her.

"Gotta go," Cammi announced, shoving the remains of her lunch back into her bag. "Carson and I are going to quiz each other on Spanish verbs after he's done playing soccer."

Aadita stood up. "I need to meet my sister to help her set up her science project. It appears that eighth-grade science is very demanding."

That left Ariana and Elizabeth. They looked at each other. There was so much to say, Ariana thought, but they had made a no-gossip pledge last year, after so many of the girls in their class had gotten, well, *mean*.

Elizabeth's invitation! How could Ariana forget? She pulled out the envelope with Elizabeth's name on it and handed it to her friend.

"What is it?" Elizabeth asked. "A party?"

"A sleepover! But I still wanted to do an invitation," Ariana explained. "That's not dumb, is it?"

"Not at all!" Elizabeth pulled out the card Ariana had worked so painstakingly on the night before. "Oh, this is so cute! I love when you rubber-stamp stuff."

"You really like it?"

"Kittens in a basket?" Elizabeth smiled. "What's not to like? It reminds me of Mrs. Herrera's ceramic kittens in her special collection, except all of your kittens have their ears!"

Ariana made a sad face. "That poor kitty cat! I wish we could fix it somehow. What was its name?"

"Sandra, maybe?" Elizabeth sounded unsure. "I think? She named it after her sister, and then her sister broke it."

"That's right. Mrs. Herrera bought them when she was only nine, the first thing she ever bought with her own money. I'm glad I don't have a mean sister like that," Ariana said. "She'd probably try to ruin my sleepover!"

"Speaking of which . . . ," Elizabeth said. "Who's invited?"

"You, of course, and Ellie Barker and Becca Hobbes,"

Ariana said, cheering again at the thought of her sleepover. "I thought it might be a nice thing to do for Becca, you know? She's been having such a hard time lately."

Elizabeth nodded. "Definitely. And I know Cammi is—well, Cammi has her own point of view. But maybe this wasn't the best time for her to, I don't know—pull away from Becca?"

"I was thinking the same thing!" Ariana said. "I mean, not judging or anything, but now's when Becca needs her friends. And since Ellie's new, I figured she might be a great person to—I don't know. Accept Becca for who she is?"

"You're exactly right," Elizabeth said. "I think we should go find Becca right now and give her the invitation."

Two minutes later they were on the playground, looking for Becca. When they finally found her, she was around the corner of the building (off-limits!), reading a book.

"What are you reading, Becca?" Ariana asked, trying to sound friendly and casual, like she was always running into Becca by herself with a book in her hand. "Anything good?"

Becca held up her book. *Salem's Lot*, by Stephen King.

"Wow! That's pretty scary stuff," Elizabeth said. "I bet it would give me nightmares."

"My mom says no Stephen King for me until high school," Ariana agreed. "My brother read a Stephen King book in seventh grade and couldn't sleep for a week!"

Becca opened her book (to a dog-eared page, Ariana noticed) and started reading again.

"I've got something for you, Becca," Ariana said, holding out the invitation. Only now she felt sort of nervous about it. She had no idea Becca had started reading horror books!

Becca glanced up. "What is it?"

"Sleepover invitation?" Ariana sounded as though she wasn't exactly sure. "I know it's kind of dumb, doing an invitation for a sleepover that's not really a party sleepover. I guess I was just feeling creative!"

"No, thanks," Becca said, not even bothering to take the envelope from Ariana.

"Come on, Becca!" Elizabeth said. "It's going to be so much fun. Me, Ariana, you, and Ellie—what could be better?"

"It's sort of a welcome-to-town party for Ellie," Ariana said, improvising on the spot. "You know, her being new and everything."

"She's weird," Becca said, her eyes still on her book. "The way she's always spying and taking notes."

Ellie's the weird one? Ariana wanted to ask, but kept her mouth shut.

"I think she's trying to find a way to fit in," Elizabeth said. She turned to Ariana and made a desperate face, like *What am I supposed to say here?*

"She's got a funny way of doing it," Becca remarked.

"Well, maybe if we make her feel welcome, she'll stop taking notes and start talking and making friends," Ariana said. "Have you ever thought of that?"

Elizabeth shot her a warning look. Had that come out too harshly?

Becca looked up again. "Quit being such a Girl Scout, Ariana. I mean, I know you *are* a Girl Scout, but you don't have to act like it all the time."

"I'm not acting," Ariana said. "I really do want to help you. I mean, help Ellie."

"Who died and made you a saint?" Becca threw

down her book and stood up. "That's what I'd really like to know. Who died and made you a saint?"

Ariana took a step backward. "That doesn't even make sense, Becca. And it's sort of funny coming from you, the world's biggest goody-goody."

"Not anymore," Becca said, smiling a scary sort of smile. "One day you'll understand—maybe when you stop acting like you're still in second grade and everything's just wonderful all the time. La-la-la, we're so perfect and sweet!"

"Well, you're a—you're a—" Ariana didn't even know what she was trying to say here, so she just kept stammering "you're a—" until finally a word came out of her mouth that she'd never said before. It was a word she'd never even thought of saying before. Oh, sure, she'd heard other girls say it, but Ariana Savarino did not use words like that. Never, ever.

She wished she could take it back!

"Ariana!" Elizabeth said in a shocked voice. "Oh my gosh!"

Becca, on the other hand, just laughed and started walking away. "See, I knew you really weren't as nice as you pretend," she called over her shoulder as she turned the corner of the building. "Maybe I'll go tell Mrs. Herrera what you just called me. Maybe everyone should know what a faker you are."

Ariana sank to the ground. How could Becca say she wasn't nice? Just because she'd gotten mad and said one bad word?

"It's okay," Elizabeth said, holding out her hand. "She's not going to tell anyone."

Ariana took Elizabeth's hand and let herself be pulled up. She'd write Becca a note of apology and mail it to her house. How could she have said such a thing?

Even if it was sort of true.

"I shouldn't have said it," she told Elizabeth. "Promise me you won't tell?"

"Of course I won't tell," Elizabeth promised as they made their way back to the playground.

By the look on everyone's face, it was clear that Elizabeth didn't need to tell anyone because Becca had already told everyone. And there she was now, talking to Mrs. Herrera!

"I think I'm going to be sick," Ariana said to

Elizabeth. "I think I need to go to the nurse's office."

"I'll take you," Elizabeth said, but Ariana noticed she'd moved away from her a little bit, like she didn't want people to think she was the kind of girl who called other girls names. Bad names.

"It's okay," Ariana told her. "I can take myself."

And then she just started running. She didn't even know where she was running to until she was in the main hallway and saw the open door to the principal's office.

"I'm turning myself in!" Ariana cried as she hurtled through the doorway. "I'm a terrible person!"

"I'm sure that's not true, Ariana," Mrs. Werter, the school secretary, said. "You're a very nice girl."

Ariana flung herself into the chair across from Mrs. Werter's desk. But she wasn't nice! She was a name-caller! She had turned into the sort of person who used bad language! She was—

Ariana actually couldn't actually think of any more bad things about herself. Just those two. And she'd said what she'd said under stress, she reminded herself. Becca really was being horrible, after all. And just because Ariana had said one bad word didn't make her un-nice, did it? Especially when—well, who was she trying to fool? Becca Hobbes sort of was—well, that thing that Ariana had called her.

Ariana took a deep breath. *So just calm down,* she told herself. *You must be turning into a teenager—so dramatic!*

"I guess maybe I'll just go back to class after all," she told Mrs. Werter, standing up. "You look very pretty today, by the way. I like your dress!"

"Why, thank you, Ariana!" Mrs. Werter said, clearly pleased by the compliment.

"You're so welcome!" Ariana replied, and then turned and headed back to Mrs. Herrera's classroom, smiling and waving at everyone she passed. Maybe she wouldn't have a party after all, she thought. Parties were overrated. Maybe it should just be Ariana and Elizabeth. They could make a list of who was nice and who wasn't and make plans for a nice people's club. That sounded like fun, didn't it? A nice people's club?

Ariana already knew who she wouldn't be inviting.

Chapter Ten

Stefan

Thursday, October 5

Since Monday and the Great Hair Escapade (as Stefan and Ben had started calling it), Mrs. Herrera had been stingy with the library passes. Cammi Lovett said it was because if one more of her students got in trouble, Mrs. Herrera would get fired. It had something to do with something that had happened last year, but no one knew for sure what it was. Matt Collins said he heard that one of her students had been sent to jail for pouring a Coke into the library aquarium and killing all the fish, but Stefan thought that was pretty unlikely, at least the jail part.

All anyone knew for sure was that Mrs. Herrera was on thin ice and seemed to be thinking twice about who she let leave the room. But on Thursday she let Petra go to the library during free period, which made everyone look around at each other with expressions that said *Really? Petra?* And when Stefan asked if he and Henry could go too, to work on their history presentation, all Mrs. Herrera said was, "Try to keep Henry on task, okay?"

Stefan nodded as he took the passes. He was used to being the kid who got paired with the troublemakers, the comedians, the ADHD types, the slow learners. He guessed he didn't mind, although he'd occasionally like to be put in a group with an actual friend as opposed to someone who needed babysitting.

His mom had gone ballistic when she'd seen this year's class list. "Carson Bennett—again? Matt Collins—again? It's like they put you in a class so there'll be one student who doesn't drive the teacher crazy."

She scrolled down the list a little farther and snorted. "Henry Lloyd—of course you're with Henry Lloyd. I bet you'll be given the seat right beside him so you can keep him under control."

"But Ben's in my class, and so is Bart," Stefan pointed out. "So I actually got some of my friends this year."

"Glad they could throw you a bone," his mom said, shutting the lid on her laptop with a decisive thud. "I'm going to go make some calls. This is unacceptable."

Stefan had grabbed her arm. "Mom! Don't! It's okay. For one thing, I don't mind. Henry's not that bad. He just doesn't know how to act around other people. Ben thinks he's on the autism spectrum or else just has serious ADHD. Besides, there are lots of really nice people in my class this year—Aadita and Ariana are the nicest girls in our grade. And I've heard Mrs. Herrera is a really good teacher."

His mom took a deep breath and closed her eyes. She let the breath out through her nose and nodded. "Okay, okay. But I'm really getting tired of this."

It was true that Henry Lloyd was the kind of kid who couldn't walk past a row of lockers without whacking each one with his notebook. But from experience, Stefan knew the best way to deal with that sort of behavior was to distract Henry, get his attention focused elsewhere.

"So do you think there are sound-absorbing panels in the ceiling?" Stefan asked on their way to the library, pointing. Sure enough, Henry quit with the notebook and looked up.

"Maybe. The question is, are they panels that absorb echoes or panels that block sound? You'd think echoes, because it's a hallway, right? Who cares if the sound goes through the ceiling? It's just a roof up there anyway."

They chatted about sound absorption versus sound blocking the rest of the way to the library. The thing that a lot of people didn't get about Henry was that he was supersmart, maybe as smart as Ben. Stefan was almost as smart as Ben—they both got taken out of regular math class to go to Mr. Lee's for pre-algebra—but certain things came easier to Ben than they did to Stefan. He had a photographic memory, which was a definite unfair advantage, and he didn't have to study very hard to get As. Stefan definitely had to study for math tests.

"I bet the library has echo-absorbing paneling,"

Henry whispered as they walked into the media center. Even Henry knew enough not to talk above a whisper around Mrs. Rosen, who wasn't a librarian who gave second chances.

"I don't know why they'd bother," Stefan pointed out. "Everybody's too afraid to talk."

Henry grinned. "She's the scariest librarian in the world."

See, Henry's not so bad, Stefan wanted to tell his mom. For that matter, neither was Carson. Carson was mostly just goofy. Matt Collins was another story. Stefan would be scared of Matt Collins, except that one time when Matt had been a jerk to him last year, Carson had stepped in and said, "Dude, this here's my little buddy. You got a problem with him, you've got a problem with me."

Embarrassing for Stefan, yes. But also a relief. He had to face facts: he was a natural target for bullies. He was short, spent most of the time with his face buried in a book, and had less than stellar hand-eye coordination. He needed somebody like Carson Bennett in his corner. And he liked Carson. He wouldn't say they were friends exactly, but they got paired together a lot, and Stefan knew he was one of the few people Carson had told about his mom's cancer. Ever since then there'd been a bond between them. An invisible bond, sure, one that nobody else really knew about, but it was real.

He and Henry sat down at a table near the back window and opened up their notebooks. They were doing a presentation on city-states in ancient Greece, focusing on the city-state of Megara, which Stefan and Henry agreed was a very cool name. That was the thing about Henry—if you could just get him to shut up and quit irritating people, he was a nice kid. Unfortunately, if you put him in a group, he was like a bouncy ball pinging around the walls, out of control. Stefan knew that there would be a huge difference between the presentation they were planning, which was both informative and interesting, and the presentation that would get presented, which would fall apart in five seconds because Henry would do something dumb, like start snapping his fingers over his head as though he was doing some Greek folk dance. That would be classic Henry.

"Dude, look—can you believe Mrs. H let her out?"

Stefan rubbed his arm where Henry had elbowed him and then looked where Henry was pointing. Petra Wilde was pulling a book off a shelf in the fiction section. Interesting. Petra seemed like more the social media type than a reader.

Of course there was the thing at Lila's party, where Petra had first talked to Ben and then climbed a tree. Ben said it wasn't any big deal, that she'd been bored and was just wandering around. Still, it had clearly been the beginning of something. The beginning of the Strangeness, Stefan thought, liking how that sounded.

"You should ask her to the sixth-grade dance," Henry said. Amazingly, he was still whispering. "Now that she's gotten so strange."

"I'm not going to the dance," Stefan whispered back, the very thought making butterflies flitter like tossed thumbtacks in his stomach. "So why would I ask anyone to go with me?"

Henry put his pencil sideways between his teeth, smiled, and rolled his eyeballs around. "Because," he said, not taking out the pencil, "she's weird, you're weird, why not be weird together?"

"But I'm not weird," Stefan insisted. He glanced nervously at Mrs. Rosen's desk. They had to be near the limit for the acceptable amount of whispering. "I'm actually quite normal."

"Uh-huh," Henry said, spitting out the pencil onto his open notebook. "Normal as me, and we both know that's not normal at all."

"We should get to work," Stefan said, not bothering to argue that he and Henry weren't anything alike. Sure, they were both smart, but Stefan actually got good grades, and Henry, unlike Stefan, was good at sports. Unlike Henry, Stefan had friends and didn't bounce off the walls or snap girls' bra straps or yell out "Cowabunga!" for no reason in the middle of Drop Everything and Read.

"Okay, but are you going to ask Petra to the dance or not?" Henry asked. "Because if you don't, I might."

"Go ahead," Stefan whispered. "I'd like to see that."

"Okay," Henry said, pushing his chair away from the table. "You've got a deal."

Stefan shook his head as he watched Henry walk over to Petra. This was going to be embarrassing. Or at the very least awkward. But then again, who knew with the new Petra, the one who kept to herself, who sat alone in the cafeteria and read a magazine while she ate? The one who Rosie had declared a total loser and untouchable, but who didn't seem to care. Yesterday Ben was talking about nuns who cut off their hair when they joined a convent, and Bart had made a joke about Sister Petra. Maybe he was onto something. Maybe Petra had joined a religious order—or a cult.

One thing was for sure: Petra Wilde may have gotten weird, but she'd never be weird enough to go to the dance with Henry.

When Henry leaned in and whispered something into Petra's ear, her left eyebrow shot up in a way Stefan thought was really cool. He wondered if she'd had to practice that in front of the mirror.

Petra looked over at Stefan. He shrugged, as if to say, *Sorry, wasn't my idea.* Petra smiled back at him, as though the two of them were in on a joke. Now Stefan felt a little light-headed. Could a smile really have that effect on a person? Make them feel like maybe they had to go to the bathroom all of a sudden?

Maybe Petra was a witch. Now there was a theory. Or maybe she was just a naturally powerful person. Everybody agreed that Becca never would have cut off her hair in the art room if Petra hadn't been with her. Had Petra really tried to convince Becca to get in trouble? Intellectually, he could understand why you might do that. What a challenge, right? How do you make the biggest goody-goody in the world go bad?

Only, Stefan wondered if Becca had already been on the road to misbehaving before Petra got ahold of her. He'd noticed Becca pouring sugar into Mrs. Herrera's desk drawer on Monday morning, and before that, he'd seen her take the caps off two dry-erase pens and put them in her pocket. It was like she was having a secret war with their teacher, but why?

It could only be the Strangeness, he thought now.

Henry crossed the library back to the table. Mrs. Rosen was also walking toward their table, so instead of saying anything, Henry turned to a fresh sheet in his notebook and wrote, *She said yes!*

Stefan grabbed Henry's pencil, completely forgetting

it had just been in Henry's mouth. *Petra's going to the dance with you?!?*

Mrs. Rosen was two tables away. Henry looked over at her, looked at Stefan, and slapped his hand over his mouth to keep from—what? Exploding, it looked like. *Not me*, Henry wrote. *She said yes she would go to the dance with YOU!!!*

And then he lost it. Just as Mrs. Rosen reached their table, Henry fell out of his seat and started rolling down the floor.

"Henry Lloyd, get off the floor and into my office!" Mrs. Rosen hissed. She turned to Stefan. "I'm very surprised at you, Stefan Morrisey! Please go back to your classroom."

Why was she surprised at him? Stefan wondered as he gathered his things. He hadn't done anything. Wasn't doing anything. Was entirely innocent of any wrongdoing.

It wasn't until he was back out in the hallway that he remembered he was going to the sixth-grade dance with Petra Wilde. But that was crazy! He barely knew Petra Wilde. Besides that, he didn't know how to dance.

She'd probably said yes as a joke, Stefan told himself. She probably didn't mean it.

He immediately felt relieved.

And disappointed.

Which was confusing.

"Hey, Stefan!" a voice called from behind him. He turned around and there she was, the Queen of the Strangeness herself.

"Hi, Petra," he stammered. "Sorry about all that. I mean, Henry and everything."

Petra looked confused. "Why are you sorry? You're the one who wanted him to ask me, right?"

"Uh, well, huh." Stefan really couldn't think of an answer here. He should just say it. Say the thing they both knew. *Be brave, my good man,* he could hear his dad saying, in his Knights of the Realm voice. "Listen, I know you said yes as a joke, and that's okay—"

"Who says I said yes as a joke? Did you ask me as a joke?"

I didn't ask you at all, Stefan almost blurted out, but he stopped himself. What if Petra was serious? He didn't want to hurt her feelings.

"No," he said, which was the truth, but only half the truth. "Did you answer as a joke?"

"No," Petra replied, and she sounded serious. "I would enjoy going to the sixth-grade dance with you. It's in two weeks, right? Because I'm thinking about making my own dress. Do you like orange?"

"Orange is nice," Stefan said.

"Okay, good," Petra said. "And Stefan?"

"Yes?"

"Thanks for asking me. I think we're going to have fun, don't you?"

She smiled at him, and Stefan felt light-headed again. "I hope so," he said. "I can't really dance, though."

"I'll teach you," she said. They'd reached Mrs. Herrera's classroom door. Petra held out her hand and Stefan took it, as though he were the sort of boy who held girls' hands every day of the week. "You just listen to the music and move to it. Sometimes it's easier if you close your eyes. Here—I'll show you."

Petra closed her eyes and started humming a song that Stefan didn't recognize. She shuffled a few steps to the left and a few steps to the right. Stefan followed her, laughing a little bit because he felt goofy dancing in the middle of the hallway, but also because it was, well, sort of fun. He was sorry when Petra stopped moving.

"You're a natural," she said, dropping his hand. "But I guess we should go in."

Stefan opened the classroom door, bowed, and said, "After you," and Petra went inside. When Stefan followed her, he found that the whole class was staring at them, their eyes full of big question marks.

"Did you lose Henry?" Mrs. Herrera asked from her desk. "Or did he get in trouble?"

"He got in trouble," Stefan said, and then he wondered if Mrs. Herrera would get fired because Henry had acted crazy in the library.

"How 'bout you, little man?" Matt called out. "You look like you're nothing but trouble."

A bunch of kids laughed at that. Stefan laughed too. He was going to the sixth-grade dance with Petra Wilde. They'd just held hands in the hallway. If that was trouble, Stefan was all for it.

Chapter Eleven

Rosie

Friday, October 6

Rosie sat by herself on the bus and stared at her phone. Petra's face stared back at her, except it didn't really look like Petra's face. Not the old Petra, at least. This new and unimproved Petra had big ears that stuck straight out and a head like a balloon. Who knew that Petra's head was so big or that her neck was so scrawny? *Good hair covers a multitude of sins,* Rosie's mom liked to say, and now Rosie knew what she meant.

How dare Petra cut her hair without discussing it with Rosie first! Not that Rosie was in charge of

Petra or controlled their friendship—their *former* friendship—but they'd been a team. They conferred about clothes and makeup and boys. They did not make rash decisions about their hair.

Rosie sighed and looked out the window. She didn't know why she was even thinking about Petra anymore. Petra was over. The problem was, lunch wasn't as much fun without Petra, and recess was boring without Petra, but the bus ride home was the worst. It was when Rosie missed her former best friend the most. They'd always spent the ten-minute ride home going over every little detail of the day—who had worn what to school, who'd had a bad hair day (ha!), which kid in their class had said the stupidest thing (not counting Carson, who said stupid stuff on purpose), who they should spend the following day making miserable.

And the best part was the secret list they were keeping about Lila, using a notebook app on Petra's phone. It actually wasn't just one list, it was an entire city of lists. Rosie's favorite one so far was called "What Lila could do with all that hair if she ever shaved her legs." Their answers included: (1) Knit a sweater; (2) Make a wig for someone with cancer; (3) Give it to the birds to build nests with; (4) Weave it into fabric to make a skirt so we wouldn't have to look at her hairy legs.

But on Wednesday, two days after she'd hacked off her hair, Petra had started riding her bike to and from school. Rosie hadn't known you could ride your bike to school, but apparently if your parents filled out a permission slip that said you would promise to stay on the bike path, it was okay. Ever since Wednesday, Petra had shown up to school with her hair (what was left of it) all messed up and her jeans stuck into her socks like she was a mentally ill person.

Usually when she got off the bus at the end of the day, Rosie felt energized even though she'd spent the last seven hours being bored to death. It was those list-making sessions with Petra that revived her. And usually Fridays were her best days, because she didn't have to do homework when she got home, so she could text with Petra and Carson and Matt, or even better, have a sleepover with Petra and text Lila about how they were soooo sorry Rosie's mom would only let her have one friend sleep over at a time.

But today, on what should be the best day of her week, Rosie felt like she needed a nap, and she never needed a nap. She almost tripped getting off the bus, and a couple of kids laughed when Mr. Melton, the bus driver, called, "Careful, young lady! You could break an ankle!"

Rosie ignored him and trudged down the sidewalk to her house.

"You want a snack?" her mom asked when Rosie came into the kitchen and threw her backpack on the table. "I just made Gabe and Garrett some graham crackers and peanut butter."

"Are you trying to make me fat?" Rosie only asked this to irritate her mom; she knew the answer was no. Her mom made a huge deal about people's weight and went to Weight Watchers every week even though she didn't need to lose a pound.

"The protein in the peanut butter balances the carbs in the graham crackers," Rosie's mother explained. "So you don't get the same sort of insulin spike you would if you'd just eaten the graham crackers by themselves."

Sometimes Rosie wondered what it was like to come

home to a mother who was just pulling a tin of blueberry muffins out of the oven. Her mom had never been that kind of mom. For the first eight years of Rosie's life, her mom had been a lawyer, and then quit when the twins were born. Just like that she went from the sort of mother who was always working and had a hard time making it to Rosie's ballet recitals on time to a mother who was obsessed with making Gabe and Garrett the smartest, healthiest, most high-achieving babies ever known to humankind.

And now she *never* made it to Rosie's ballet recitals. The twins weren't good with babysitters. "Aunt Maggie is going, and she looks just like me," her mom always said. "So everyone will think your mom's there!"

Aunt Maggie and Rosie's mom were twins too, and they did look a lot alike. But having someone who looked like your mom in the audience wasn't the same as having your actual mom in the audience. And Rosie's dad never came to anything because he was always out of town. Rosie was starting to suspect he traveled so much because he didn't really like their family. Neither did she, actually, but she was stuck at home until she was eighteen whether she liked her family or not.

Oh well, Rosie thought as she grabbed a cup of yogurt from the fridge. She was planning on quitting ballet after this year anyway, so it wouldn't matter who did or didn't show up at her recitals, because she wouldn't be there either.

"I'm going upstairs to FaceTime with—" Rosie almost said Petra, because that was another thing they did on Friday, video chat as soon as they got home to make weekend plans. Rosie had to remind herself she wouldn't be caught dead FaceTiming with Petra anymore. "Lila—I'm going to FaceTime with Lila."

"Oh, honey, I need you to look after the twins. It's only for thirty minutes, but I didn't make it to the store earlier, and if I don't go now, I don't know what we'll do for dinner."

"Order a pizza," Rosie suggested as she grabbed her backpack from the table. "The twins love pizza."

"Yeah, but my rear end doesn't, and yours won't either. You can chat with your friends in the living room. The twins are watching TV."

Rosie sighed. The problem with having a former

attorney for a mother was there was no point in arguing with her, because you couldn't win. Rosie carried her yogurt and her phone into the next room. Gabe and Garrett were watching something idiotic on Nickelodeon, a channel Rosie's old nanny, Amy, had never let her watch. Amy was pretty much against TV in general; she liked taking walks or playing soccer or helping Rosie practice for her dance recitals.

"Rosie Posie!" Gabe squealed when he saw her. "Can I sit on your lap?"

"No, you can't," Rosie told him. "And you can't call me Rosie Posie, either. It's stupid."

"But I'm smart," Gabe said. "I can read."

"No, you can't. Recognizing a stop sign isn't the same as reading."

"I can read too!" Garrett chimed in. "Stop! Green light! Go!"

Rosie sank into the couch, ignoring her brothers, the two most annoying three-year-olds on the face of the planet. Hi, Lila! she texted. What's the Petra report for today? I still don't get her eating lunch with Stefan. Lower your standards much?

Next, to Matt Collins: I saw you staring at Lila today. Are you in loooovvvve?

To Garrison: I heard Mrs. Herrera has two drunk driving charges on her license, and that's why she's going to get fired soon.

To Carson: My life is SO boring.

Then she waited. Of course Lila, Miss Overeager Pleaser, texted back two seconds later. How low can you go, right? I mean, Stefan? Why not date a hamburger?

Rosie rolled her eyes. Wha??

I mean, Stefan practically is a hamburger, right?

He's okay, Rosie texted. We were friends in preschool.

I thought you said he reads too much.

I thought we were talking about Petra.

Ping! A text from Matt scrolled across the top of the screen. Lila!?!? UR NUTS!!!!

Rosie didn't bother replying. Matt was boring. She tried Carson again. How's travel soccer going? I heard you were playing striker.

Lila again. Petra smelled bad today. Like she was having stomach problems.

You mean like farts? If you mean farts, just say farts.

Yeah. Definitely farts!

Gabe turned up the TV. "Turn it down, or I'll turn it down for you!" Rosie commanded.

"Rosie Posie is a nosey toesey!" Gabe said with a pout. But he turned down the TV.

My brothers suck, she wrote Lila. Why couldn't I have a sister?

I have a little sister, Lila texted back. She's okay, but she picks her nose.

You're all about the body stuff, aren't you? Farts, boogers. Sort of gross, Lila!

Why oh why did Petra have to go insane? Rosie wondered, leaning back against the couch cushions. She used to be so funny, and not fart and booger funny, either. Mean funny. It was like Petra could look at people and know their secrets. "Matt Collins is afraid of heights," she'd observed one day at the pool last summer. "I'll give you ten dollars if you ever see him go off the diving board or down the slide." According to Petra, Carson played dumb because he was afraid he really *was* dumb, Garrison hardly ever talked because he was scared his voice would crack, and Cammi Lovett wore baggy shirts because she'd developed breasts over the summer—real ones. Petra knew which girls had actually started their periods and which ones said they had but hadn't.

What happened to that Petra? Where did she go? Who was the girl in class today who called herself Petra but was someone else entirely? Rosie had actually overheard Petra asking Elizabeth Hernandez if she was interested in collecting clothes for kids who lived in some homeless shelter over near the mall.

"It's my mom's deal," Petra had told Elizabeth. "She's kind of a professional do-gooder. Really—she used to work for United Way. Now she volunteers a hundred hours a week at the shelter."

Elizabeth's face had gone all red and splotchy. "Uh, wow, that would be—collecting clothes would be—"

"Awesome, right?" Petra had finished for her. "If you could make some posters, I'll bring in some collection bins. Mrs. Herrera said it would be okay."

Clothes for the homeless? Okay, great, sure. Homeless people needed clothes like everybody else, Rosie guessed. But the old Petra wouldn't have touched somebody else's used and probably still dirty old clothes for a million dollars. *Girl Scout work,* she would have called it.

So when had Petra Wilde become a Girl Scout?

I miss the old Petra, she started to text Lila, but Lila wouldn't get it. Lila was scared of Petra and glad that Petra had become the class weirdo. Rosie deleted the text. What she needed to do was get the old Petra back, the one with good hair and a mean sense of humor. Maybe if Rosie went into school on Monday and slapped Petra really hard, Petra would get over herself. *Snap out of it, Petra!* she'd yell, and Petra's eyes would open superwide, like she'd been a zombie for a while, but Rosie's slap had awakened her.

Of course, if she slapped Petra, she'd be automatically suspended from school. Besides, Rosie didn't like drama—not loud, dramatic drama anyway. No, she needed a quieter plan, one that would appeal to Petra's sneaky, devious side. She needed a plan that would remind Petra of how fun it was to be mean.

What could Rosie do that was subtle, yet would get Petra's attention? It would have to be at school, because

Insane Petra probably wouldn't come over to her house (and honestly, Rosie didn't want Insane Petra in her house), and it would have to be something that would cause a stir, but not a commotion. Nothing overly dramatic or crazy. Nothing that would make Henry Lloyd do backflips and start shouting nonsense words.

Rosie closed her eyes. She pictured Mrs. Herrera's classroom. Desks, book nook, Editor's Roundtable, Mrs. Herrera's desk and bookshelf—Rosie stopped. Mrs. Herrera's bookshelf, where Mrs. Herrera kept her special collection of special things. "These things remind me of why I want to teach," Mrs. Herrera had told them the first day of school, and Rosie and Petra had looked at each other and pretended to gag. The things on the shelf weren't that great—a stupid book, a stupid picture of some supposedly awesome teacher Mrs. Herrera had when she was in high school, her father's junior high diploma, and a bunch of other junk. A football, some sugar cubes. Stupid. But the more Rosie thought about the shelf, the more she was sure the answer was there. Rosie had to lure the old Petra back with an example of good, mean fun, and what better than to do something that would make Mrs. Herrera go all *Woe is me* and start sniffling and snorting and telling the class about how special her special things were and how everything was meaningful, boo hoo!

Meet me at school early on Monday, she texted Lila. **Get your mom to drive you so that you're there before the buses get there. I'll be waiting.**

Because Rosie wasn't going to do the dastardly deed herself, of course.

That's what other people were for.

Chapter Twelve

Ethan
Monday, October 9

Ethan checked for Rogan and Cole as soon as he walked into the cafeteria at lunchtime, making sure they were sitting at their usual table. Sometimes they got kicked over to another table by a group of eighth-grade football players, but no, there they were, same old place, unwrapping their sandwiches. Cool. The Trio of Trouble needed to have a serious discussion about how they were going to track down whoever stole the special things from Mrs. Herrera's special collection. The thief *would* be caught, and he—or she—*would* be brought to justice.

Ethan waved at his friends with his lacrosse stick and started toward the table, stopping as always to say hi to Stefan, Ben, and Bart. Well, mostly he was saying hi to Stefan, who lived on Ethan's street and was kind of like family—like a cousin or something. They didn't hang out much anymore, and Stefan had never been a lot of fun to begin with (you had to pull him out of a book to get him to do anything), but family was family, and it was important to keep in touch.

"My mom said Mr. Rylant fell and broke his hip on Saturday," Ethan told Stefan as he waved his stick at Ben and Bart. "She's going to start a meal train on SignUp.com."

"That sucks," Stefan said. "I mean about Mr. Rylant. I saw him out walking Sporty Saturday morning."

Ethan nodded. "Yeah, Sporty's a good dog."

He didn't have anything else to say, so he waved his stick again and headed over to his table. On the way, he passed Cammi and Carson sitting together, their Spanish books open in front of them. Normally, he wouldn't stop to talk, but Carson looked up as Ethan was right by their table and said, "Dude, pass me the ball!"

"No ball in this pocket, dog," Ethan said. "Not allowed in the cafeteria."

"I'm surprised they let you carry your stick in here," Cammi said, and Ethan felt like telling her that *he* was surprised to see her hanging out with Carson Bennett instead of Becca Hobbes, but what did he care? He wasn't into labels, anyway, all this *who's popular, who's not.* All he cared about was the stick in his hand—and finding out who stole Mrs. Herrera's stuff.

"So have you heard any rumors about what happened to Mrs. H's special things?" he asked, tossing the stick from one hand to the other. "Because I think it sucks that there's, like, a thief in our classroom."

Carson shrugged. "You got me, dude. I mean, it's not like any of it was worth anything. So why steal it?"

"Yeah," Cammi agreed. "What's the motivation?"

"Exactly," Carson said, nodding like Cammi had said something brilliant. "Motivation is key here."

"Cool," Ethan said, and waved his stick at them before heading over to his table.

* * *

Ethan was no stranger to bad news. Like when he learned that Luke was going to play goalie on the Comets, the region's best lacrosse travel team in the thirteen-and-under league? It had taken him a week to recover after he heard that. And when he saw the class list and realized he was going to have to put up with Henry Lloyd for another year, he'd eaten a whole bag of Fritos. Henry drove him crazy. Henry drove everybody crazy except for Stefan, who must have had special superpowers to put up with Henry as much as he did.

But when he heard that Mrs. Herrera's signed copy of *Hatchet* had been stolen? It was like someone had punched Ethan in the gut.

"A number of things from my special collection are missing, including my signed copy of *Hatchet*," Mrs. Herrera had announced Monday in LA, right before lunch, and everybody in the class started going *What— what—what?* at the same time. Not Ethan, though. It wasn't that he wasn't as shocked as everyone else. It was just that he thought he might cry.

He loved *Hatchet*.

He even sort of loved Mrs. Herrera. Not romantically—dude, gross—but as a teacher he didn't hate. Which of course meant she was about to get fired, because that was the kind of luck Ethan seemed to be having lately. He finally got a teacher he actually liked and it turned out she had some sort of criminal past. Ariana said she'd helped one of her students run away from home, that it was a big secret that a lot a people knew about, but that the court documents had been sealed. Rogan said there was no way that had happened, that Mrs. Herrera would have already been fired by now if it had, but why would Ariana make something like that up? Ethan was pretty sure that any day now Mrs. Herrera was going to get sacked.

Which was just his luck.

Until this year, school had been a total waste of time. Ethan figured that everything they were trying to teach him was available 24/7 on his phone, so why should he bother learning it? Besides, he was going to be a professional lacrosse player, so he didn't actually need an education. But his mom kept making him go to school, day after boring day, and sometimes Ethan thought that if he had to sit in a stupid classroom one more second, he might explode, his blood and guts flying all over the place and splotching up the windows.

But this year school finally got interesting. There was the weirdness with Becca and Petra, for one thing. Not that they'd become friends or anything, but when they gave each other those bad haircuts like some sort of practical joke? Awesome! Next, there was a rumor that Stefan and Petra were going to the dance together—how freakishly cool was that?

And Mrs. Herrera was a pretty decent teacher. She let them talk about sports for the first five minutes of homeroom class every Monday, and she was a big Cleveland Browns fan. Ethan wasn't, but he respected that she had a team. He thought her little football was cool, even though he'd had to look up who Jim Brown was. But that was okay, because Jim Brown was totally cool and now Ethan knew all about him if the subject ever came up. And Mrs. Herrera wasn't too boring, at least not most of the time. Okay, sometimes when she was teaching stuff in LA like verbs and how to write a good paragraph, things got kind of snoozy. But mostly

Ethan could halfway deal with her, and that was saying a lot.

Maybe Ethan wouldn't have cared so much about somebody stealing *Hatchet*, but *Hatchet* was the only book he'd ever actually liked. Okay, loved. The book they'd been reading in class, *Wonder*, was okay, but that Auggie kid was way too strange. Not just his face, but his super-annoying positive attitude. Brian in *Hatchet*? Totally awesome.

"When I was in college studying to be a teacher, Gary Paulsen came to a class I was taking in children's literature," Mrs. Herrera had told Ethan before handing him a copy of the book (not her autographed copy, but the one from the book nook). "He made a huge impression on me, not only as a writer, but as a human being who lived a fascinating and valuable life. I know you say you don't like to read, but I think you would enjoy this book."

Then she told him a bunch of interesting stuff, like the fact that Gary Paulsen was really into sled-dog racing, and how some man had tried to kidnap him when he was a kid, so his mom beat the guy to death. After that, Ethan couldn't wait to start the book, a feeling he'd never had before in his life.

Ethan read *Hatchet* in, like, three hours. It was awesome. And the next day he asked Mrs. Herrera if he could look at her autographed copy, and she'd let him. She didn't even say the usual teacher stuff, like *Be very careful* or *Are your hands clean?* It was like she trusted him with it because she knew he'd totally gotten into the book. She knew he wasn't going to drop it or throw it across the room at Cole.

So now he was bummed. In fact, Ethan felt like he'd been punched in the gut. When Mrs. Herrera had told the class that *Hatchet* had been stolen, his hand had shot into the air. "We'll get *Hatchet* back for you, Mrs. Herrera!" he'd practically shouted, his voice all emotional. "We'll figure out who committed this crime!"

By *we* he meant Rogan, Cole, and himself. The Trio of Trouble.

"It was Becca Hobbes," Rogan said as soon as Ethan sat down. "Obviously. Only, Cole here disagrees with me."

"It's *too* obvious," argued Cole, who as always was drawing something in his sketchbook. "I mean, at least now that Becca's gotten all strange. You know who I think did it? Ariana. Because she's the last person in the world you'd think would do it. Becca used to be that person, but now she's prime suspect numero uno, and the prime suspect never ends up being the one who's done the crime."

He held up his drawing of Ariana wearing a burglar's mask and carrying a sack filled with stuff over her shoulder.

"Dude, nice. But what's Ariana's motive?" Ethan asked, feeling like Sherlock Holmes (and a little like Cammi Lovett). "Why would she do it?"

"She wants to get everyone to quit talking about how she called Becca a—you know," Cole replied. "And she knows, given how Becca's been acting lately, that everyone will think Becca did it. It's called subterfuge, my friend."

Ethan shook his head. "Nah, Ariana wouldn't risk it. Because if she got caught, then she'd have to hand over her Queen of the Nice Girls crown."

"Yeah, I'm with Ethan here," Rogan said. "Ariana's got too much to lose. So how about Petra?"

"Old Petra, sure," Cole said. "New Petra? I don't think so."

Ethan agreed. "It's like she traded in her meanness for . . . I don't know. Something else."

"A space alien suit," Rogan supplied. "The only reason I'd go to the middle-school dance is to see her there with Stefan."

They all cracked up at that.

"Hey, maybe Stefan did it!" Cole exclaimed, and they cracked up some more.

Ethan looked over where Ariana, Elizabeth, and Aadita were eating lunch. He didn't know why he and Rogan and Cole were mostly focused on girls when the thief was probably Henry. Henry was famous for doing dumb, super-irritating things. Stealing Mrs. Herrera's favorite book would be right up his alley.

But when his eyes landed on Ellie Barker, a new thought came to Ethan's brain. Ellie was kind of this mystery girl, always taking notes and hanging around different groups of people without actually joining in.

Plus, she liked to read, and he'd seen her standing next to Mrs. Herrera's special collection of special things a lot. It was like she couldn't take her eyes off it.

But why would Ellie steal a copy of *Hatchet*? Or those three little kittens (including the one with the broken ear)? What would she do with that picture of Mrs. Herrera's favorite teacher? None of it made sense to Ethan. Well, maybe stealing *Hatchet*—in spite of what Carson thought, it was probably super valuable. But the other stuff was junk.

Ellie Barker. Ethan nodded his head slowly. Other than Aadita, she was the last person in the world who anyone would suspect. And that was why Ethan suspected her. Now all he had to do was figure out where she'd hidden the goods. Now all he had to do was spy on the spy.

"Hey, guys, I've got an idea," he said to Rogan and Cole, and the Trio of Trouble leaned in and started to make a plan.

Chapter Thirteen

Ellie

Monday, October 9

If Ellie had stolen goods to hide, the baseball field dugouts were where she would hide them, which was why she'd spent the last few minutes of recess nosing around the home-team side. She could imagine taping *Hatchet* underneath one of the long benches, or digging a hole in the dirt and burying the three little ceramic kittens. As for the picture of Mrs. Herrera's favorite teacher, well, Ellie didn't know how you'd hide that in a dugout. Maybe you'd put it right out in the open, figuring that no one came out here in the fall anyway, so why bother hiding it? It wasn't like anyone else was going to want it even if they did find it.

She figured whoever had taken the special things was pulling a prank and had hidden the booty until they could return it without being seen. She was hoping to get a peek into Henry's locker later that afternoon, because he was the most obvious prankster in their class and the person with the least self-control, but for now she was running her hand under the dugout bench. Her hand touched something hard and bumpy, and when she leaned down to get a look, she found a humongous wad of dried gum under the bench. How did anyone fit that much gum in their mouth? It made Ellie's jaw hurt just imagining it.

She was about to cross the field to the other dugout when a voice came from behind the dugout wall. "Quit!" somebody (a boy) hissed. This was followed by a thump—like someone stumbling into the dugout—and the sound of shushing.

Okay, so what should she do here? Run for the school building? Hide in the corner? Or just casually walk over to the other dugout like she hadn't heard anything?

Ellie chose to walk. She wasn't doing anything wrong, and if someone was thinking about beating her up or pushing her or—what? Spitting on her? Yelling at her? Tripping her?—it wasn't like she couldn't yell and one of the playground monitors wouldn't hear her. The school building wasn't *that* far away.

But no one jumped out or started chasing her as she walked across the pitcher's mound toward the away-team dugout. She knew she'd heard at least two people outside the dugout wall; she wasn't crazy. As a spy, Ellie could appreciate other spies, especially ones who apparently had no interest in beating her up. She smiled at the idea that someone might find her interesting enough to spy on.

But what if the other spies were doing the same thing Ellie was? What if they were looking for Mrs. Herrera's special things? What if the spies thought Ellie was the thief and hoped she would lead them to the stolen items?

Now Ellie felt like every step she took looked suspicious. She started to zigzag to throw the potential spy off her path, but realized that if normal walking looked suspicious, then zigzagging would look crazy. Besides, she wasn't in a crowded airport, where zigzagging to throw someone off your path made sense. She was crossing a baseball field.

Okay, but what if the spies didn't consider her a suspect? What if they were smart enough to realize that Ellie was looking for Mrs. Herrera's missing special objects and planned on swooping in when Ellie finally found them? She'd do all the hard work and the other spies would take the prize. Totally unfair!

She turned toward the main building and tried to walk as casually as she could, like, *Hey, no big deal, just out taking my lunchtime walk.* And then super-duper casually, she glanced behind her to see if she could get a glimpse of whoever was watching her. A dark-haired head ducked behind the dugout. So she really hadn't been imagining things! But who did the head belong to? Bart? He had dark brown hair. But Bart never came outside at recess. He and Ben and Stefan always went to the computer lab.

When she reached the blacktop, she thought about standing there and waiting for the spies to reveal themselves. But Charlotte was hanging out by the swings with some other girls from her class, and when she saw Ellie she waved, and Ellie waved back, and then Ellie didn't know what to do next, so she looked at her feet. She wondered if she should go over and say hi. Maybe invite Charlotte to her house after school? Could she do that? Back when Ellie's dad was in the army, everybody invited everybody over whether you were new or just about to move, but civilian life was different. It had different rules.

By the time she looked up again, Charlotte and the other girls were walking toward the school building, and the playing fields were one big blank space. Mrs. Herrera was standing by the basketball hoop, talking to Mrs. Kafsky. Did Mrs. Kafsky know why Mrs. Herrera was on thin ice? Ellie definitely didn't think Mrs. Herrera had been caught driving drunk like some people were saying. Not only wasn't Mrs. Herrera the drunk-driving type, but Ellie had asked her dad about it and he'd looked up the state laws about grounds for dismissing a teacher and said Mrs. Herrera would have definitely been fired immediately if she'd been arrested for driving under the influence of alcohol.

"Any sort of conviction, even a misdemeanor, would have probably gotten Mrs. Herrera terminated," her dad told her when they'd talked about it at dinner a few nights ago. "So my guess is if she's really on thin ice, it's for a pattern of behavior that isn't actually actionable."

"English, please," Ellie had told her dad, who tended to talk like a lawyer when it came to legal matters.

"She's not breaking the rules, but she keeps doing something that really irritates the school administration."

So really, there were two sixth-grade mysteries to figure out, but Ellie wasn't making a dent in either of them. She decided to focus for now on who had taken the things from Mrs. Herrera's special collection. Maybe if she could figure out who had followed her to the dugout, she'd come across an important clue. *Use your brain,* she told herself. *Use your powers of deduction. Okay, okay, okay. Who would think of following me to see if I was the thief?* Computer lab boys: probably not, because they probably didn't care. Popular boys:

nope, too cool to care. That left the nice boys who didn't overlap with the computer lab boys: Rogan, Ethan, and Cole.

She looked over to the basketball court. No sign of any of those guys. They weren't hanging around on the monkey bars either.

They were the ones outside the dugout, Ellie decided. *And I bet they suspect I did it. But why?*

She needed to write in her notebook to think this through, so she ran as fast as she could to Mrs. Herrera's classroom, where she'd dropped her backpack before lunch. But when she got there, the door was locked. What was that about? Mrs. Herrera never locked her door!

But until today, no one had stolen any of her special things from her special collection, Ellie reminded herself. *Until today, Mrs. Herrera trusted us.*

She pressed her face against the door's narrow window. Was Mrs. Herrera in there, grading papers? Had she locked herself in while she locked everyone else out? Ellie didn't see her at her desk or wiping the morning's lessons off the whiteboard. And then it occurred to her that—duh!—she'd just seen her teacher on the playground talking to Mrs. Kafsky.

But who was that boy sitting at the Editor's Round-table, scribbling away in a notebook? Sam Hawkins? What in the heck was Sam doing in Mrs. Herrera's locked classroom? She tapped on the glass and called, "Sam! I thought you moved! Are you back?"

Sam looked up, quickly closed his notebook, and pushed his chair away from the table so that he was out of view. Ellie craned her neck, but it was no use. He'd disappeared.

Ellie stood another moment, wondering what she should do. Bang on the door and force Sam to let her in? Find Mrs. Herrera and ask her what Sam was doing back in their classroom? Mrs. Herrera had to know, right?

Wait a minute—maybe Sam was the thief!

No, Ellie thought, shaking her head. That didn't make any sense. He wouldn't be locked in Mrs. Herrera's classroom without her knowing about it, and Mrs. Herrera wouldn't leave him there alone if she suspected he'd taken her things.

Okay, question one: How long had Sam been hanging out in Mrs. Herrera's classroom? Ellie had seen him a week ago, the day that Petra and Becca had cut their hair, walking into the school when everyone else was walking out. And a couple of other kids had seen him around as well. Carson, for one, and Ariana for another. Maybe Henry had spent most of Friday chanting, "I do not like green eggs and ham, Sam I am" because he'd seen Sam too. But no one had said they'd seen Sam in the middle of the day, in Mrs. Herrera's classroom.

Ellie's fingers itched, she needed a notebook so badly.

She scooched down the hall to her locker, where she had several spare notebooks stored, in case of emergency. Then she made her way to the library, found her favorite table by the far window, and plopped down. Where was her pen? Found it. Okay, she had several mysteries to work out, in no particular order.

(1) What was Sam Hawkins doing locked in Mrs. Herrera's classroom? And why had he hidden when Ellie saw him?

(2) Why would Rogan and Ethan and Cole think

she'd stolen Mrs. Herrera's special objects? They'd have to rule out a lot of other people, including Henry. Poor Henry, Ellie thought. He really wasn't a bad guy, he was just so hyper! The question was, if Henry had stolen Mrs. Herrera's things, could he have gone all morning without blurting out a confession? Unlikely. So it was smart to rule him out.

She'd heard a lot of people whispering about Becca Hobbes, but Ellie had seen Becca's face when Mrs. Herrera had made the announcement, and she'd looked genuinely surprised. Pleased, but surprised. She'd bet those guys had ruled Becca out too.

(3) So if she hadn't stolen Mrs. Herrera's special things, and none of those other people had stolen Mrs. Herrera's special things, then who the heck had stolen Mrs. Herrera's special things?

Ellie leaned back in her chair. Was this the hook for her novel? A theft in the classroom? A hidden boy?

She'd been studying the members of Mrs. Herrera's homeroom class for two weeks now. She still didn't have all the information she wanted for her book—Felicity remained a mystery to her, and Aadita was impossible to get to know—but she had a lot more than she used to. She knew, for instance, that Carson's mom was in remission from cancer (she'd overheard him tell Stefan that his mom still had "chemo brain" even though she was done with chemotherapy). She knew that Ariana was in Girl Scouts and collected Disney figurines, and that Rogan's dad was one-quarter Japanese and his mother was a professional organizer. Cole hated coleslaw, but he loved mashed potatoes, and his favorite books were comic books. Cammi loved scary stories and fantasy novels, and as far as Ellie could tell, she loved Carson, too. Or at least she liked him a lot. Interestingly, Carson sort of seemed like he liked Cammi back, although they were in different categories of people, categories (nice versus popular) that didn't usually overlap.

So maybe Cammi was the thief? Maybe she was trying to impress Carson? But would Carson really care?

Maybe Lila did it! Maybe Lila did it because . . .

Ellie didn't know why Lila would have stolen Mrs. Herrera's special things. But that was okay, because she'd figure it out while she was writing her story.

But what about the Sam Hawkins mystery? How could she get to the bottom of *that*? She had no information, no leads, no theories. All she had was a series of observations—her own and a couple of other kids'—that Sam was back, but back in a sneaky, mysterious sort of way.

Well, observations were a start, Ellie decided. Now it was time to look for actual clues. And to start writing.

It was a dark and stormy morning, she wrote, and then crossed it out. *The day started the way every day did, except this day was different.* Nope, nope.

No one knew who did it, but Ellie Barker was going to find out.

No one knew why the boy was back, but Ellie Barker was going to find out.

Yes! That was it. That was her beginning.

Now all she had to find out was what happened next.

Chapter Fourteen

HENRY

Tuesday, October 10

By Tuesday one thing was absolutely clear: everybody thought Henry did it.

They didn't have to say it, although obviously they were saying it. In fact, they were saying it to Henry's face, just so there wouldn't be any confusion.

"Just give the stuff back," Rosie told him on the way to history, poking her pencil in his shoulder. "I'm really sick of hearing about it every single second of the day."

"I didn't take it," Henry protested, rubbing his shoulder where the eraser had pushed against it. "So how can I give it back?"

"Just figure it out, idiot."

How was he supposed to figure it out? How could he figure out how to return stolen goods when he, in fact, had not stolen them? He had no magic machine, no app, no powers of persuasion to make disappeared objects reappear.

By the time he reached Mrs. Hulka's room, Henry was starting to bounce on the balls of his feet. Did he need to pee? Maybe he needed to pee. He would ask if he could go pee, only he wouldn't say "pee." He'd say, *May I please use the receptacles in the restroom facilities, the ones with the flushing apparatuses attached, oh ye wise history teacher? Could I please miss five minutes of your brilliant and very interesting class?*

He wondered if he'd find Sam I Am Green Eggs and Ham in the bathroom again, like he had on Friday morning. "You didn't see me," Sam had said as he brushed past Henry on his way out the door, but Henry *had* seen him. Sam I Am had been right in front of his face. Still, Henry decided not to say anything. He could keep a secret. Besides, who would believe him? Sure, they believed Carson, and they believed Ariana when they'd said they'd seen Sam, but Henry? No way, Josie. Henry was unbelievable.

Which was why no one believed he was innocent of this Very Major Crime of stealing Mrs. Herrera's Very Special Things.

"Henry, take a seat up front where I can keep my eye on you," Mrs. Hulka called when she saw him. "Did you do your homework?"

"I did, but the goldfish ate it," Henry replied. He sat down and pulled last night's completely completed assignment out of his notebook and started folding it into a paper airplane. Maybe he'd turn it in, maybe he wouldn't. What would he get in exchange if he did? He missed the days of smiley-face stickers on your homework sheets. *I would like to be a smiley-face sticker when I grow up*, Henry thought, which made him laugh out loud—barking, hiccupy laughs.

"Dude, shut it!" Matt Collins, who was sitting behind Henry, thwacked him in the back with his notebook. "Quit being such a freaking freak all the time!"

Henry twirled around in his seat. "It was you, wasn't it? You stole the little kittens. Did you want to give them some mittens?"

"Shut up, weirdo! Everyone knows you stole Mrs. Herrera's stuff!"

Stefan, who was sitting in the desk next to Henry, leaned over and whispered, "Henry, focus. Eyes front and center. Do a meditation moment like we do in LA."

Henry turned back around and looked straight ahead. He took a deep breath and let it out. He loved it when Mrs. Herrera did meditation moments. He loved getting to close his eyes in the middle of the day and just breathe, everybody else around him just breathing too. It was the only time his brain ever relaxed.

He heard Mrs. Hulka whisper, "Thank you, Stefan," which broke the spell. "Enough breathing!" he exclaimed. "I demand that we all stop breathing."

Mrs. Hulka sighed. "Okay, everyone, let's get started, shall we?"

Translation: *Everybody ignore Henry.*

Sure, ignore Henry unless you want to accuse him of stealing stuff. Then, hey, everybody, pay attention to Henry! Henry ground his pencil lead into his homework sheet. He'd never stolen anything, ever! He'd never stolen, burglarized, shoplifted, jaywalked, or even murdered a flea. Not even a flea! Yes, okay, he liked pulling pranks, but his pranks were not felonious. He, Henry Lloyd, was un-arrestable because he'd never broken the law. Not once. Not in the least.

"Henry, please stop tapping your pencil on your desk," Mrs. Hulka said. "You're distracting your classmates."

Henry turned around so he could see who looked distracted. Matt looked half-asleep. Ellie the spy was writing spy notes in her blue notebook, the one she carried with her all the time. What was she writing about? What amazing secrets was she inscribing into her super-special cerulean-blue spy notebook? What was she noting? Henry had to know. Not that he would consider stealing Ellie's notebook, but he would consider borrowing it. Yes, when the opportunity arose, Henry would borrow Ellie's notebook and read all her secret observations. He wouldn't tell anybody what he'd read, though. He could keep a secret. He was keeping the secret of Sam, wasn't he?

And he was keeping the secret of Becca Hobbes, who was trying so hard to be bad, but was so bad at being bad. She was better at being sad, Henry thought. That was her secret. He'd found her in her new hideout around the side of the school (he was very good at finding people who didn't want to be found), reading a book and crying.

"Why the tears, Pierre?" Henry had asked. "You can tell me. I'm your avenging angel, a highly regarded defender of damsels in distress."

He had expected Becca to throw her book at him, but instead she looked at him and asked, "Did you ever lose your best friend?"

"Strictly speaking, I never had a best friend," Henry admitted. "But it would be a loss to lose one."

"Now I wonder if I ever had a best friend either," Becca said, her expression transforming into a scowling emoji face. "She knew I liked Carson! So now she's all buddy-buddy with him?"

"You like Carson?" Henry shook his head. Becca and Carson were a terrible match. They'd end up in divorce court, befuddled by their poor spouse-choosing skills.

Becca stared down at her book. "Don't tell, okay? It was stupid. Why would Carson ever like me?"

Henry bowed low and tipped his invisible hat. "*Au contraire!* It is you who are too good for that scoundrel."

And then he sealed his lips. Lipped his seals. Spoke nary a word to nary a soul.

Yes, indeedy, Henry Lloyd could keep a secret. Why, just ask Mrs. H, who had let not one but two students take a day off last year for special research projects. One of those students just happened to be Henry's neighbor, Lucy Yee, who had gone to the zoo to write a poem about giraffes. Lucy's own mother had participated in the ruse, but VP Whalen had not been amused. Paperwork had not been filled out and permission had not been given. Mom says okay? Too bad. Not good enough.

And then it turned out Mrs. Herrera had let another student do almost the exact same thing earlier in the year, take a day off school without official permission. There was your thin ice right there, sports fans. Not that Henry would ever tell.

Who would believe him anyway?

His chance to steal Ellie's notebook came right before the end of class. Mrs. Hulka said that anyone who had a question about their upcoming project should come see her at her desk. Ellie closed her blue notebook, put it under her green notebook (this girl had ten quintillion notebooks, maybe eleven quintillion!), and went to stand in line behind Elizabeth and Aadita. Ah, Aadita. If only she would eat a hamburger, Henry would marry her. But he feared her vegetarian ways would get in the way of their marital bliss. Still, he loved saying her name, which sounded a lot like Adidas, his favorite brand of shoe.

Getting up from his desk, he held out his pencil like a white flag. An upraised pencil signaled *Don't be afraid! All I'm doing is walking to the back of the classroom to use the sharpener! No hijinks happening here!*

But be very afraid if you're Ellie's supersecret spy notebook, Henry thought as he began his journey down the aisle. He swung his left arm in a wide arc. Just old Henry being goofy. Just Henry expending a little excess energy. And what's that on Ellie's desk? Oh nothing, oh don't even bother watching as Henry's hand reaches down and plucks Ellie's notebook and tucks it under his arm. What notebook? That notebook? That's my notebook, why do you ask?

He glanced around, but nobody was paying attention

to him. Henry resisted the urge to start singing or fall to the floor and do somersaults all the way to the pencil sharpener. He reached the back of the room, sharpened his pencil, and went back to his desk, where he immediately deposited Ellie's notebook into his backpack.

A little light reading for this evening, he thought right as the bell rang. He wondered if Ellie had written about him, and if so, what? Did she think he was the thief? Well, someone like Ellie would demand proof, Henry thought as he dropped his freshly sharpened pencil into his backpack. She would demand he be tried by a jury of his peers and that evidence be presented against him before a ruling could be made.

"Henry, I want that homework assignment turned in tomorrow," Mrs. Hulka called out as he headed for the door. For a brief moment, Henry thought about plucking his homework—i.e., his newest paper airplane—out of his pack and sailing it in Mrs. Hulka's direction. Here you are! Enjoy!

But he didn't. Because his mind was already out the door and headed for LA. And his feet were headed for the bathroom—he really had to pee, Sam or no Sam.

His hands were slapping the lockers as he passed them, *bang-bang-bang.* His nose was sniffing the air, sniffing that smell of the cafeteria cranking up for lunch and the piney scent of the janitor's bucket and the ever-present odor of wet paper towels (why did school smell so much like wet paper towels?). His mind? His mind was thinking about what he would find in Ellie's notebook.

He hoped he would find himself.

He hoped Ellie knew he didn't do it.

Chapter Fifteen

Lila

Wednesday, October 11

"How could you lose a photograph?" Rosie asked when Lila finally confessed her crime at lunch on Wednesday. "It was in a frame. It was virtually unlosable unless you're a complete idiot."

"I don't know," Lila said. She crammed a handful of grapes in her mouth, feeling desperate. "It was in my backpack on Monday afternoon, and then when I got home, it wasn't."

"So then you're a complete idiot," Rosie said, sticking her spoon into her yogurt. "No big surprise there. Listen, you need to find it. If you don't, then I'm going to have to report I saw you taking something from Mrs. Herrera's shelf."

Lila was stunned. "Why would you do that? It doesn't even make any sense that you would do that."

"Well, you did steal it, didn't you?" Now Rosie was examining the yogurt on her spoon as though it were something strange and foreign. She stuck the spoon back into the container without taking a bite. "Sooner or later, someone should tell Mrs. Herrera."

"But it was your idea!" Lila felt like crying. This was so unfair! "Why should I get in trouble for something that you told me to do?"

"The way I remember it, it was your idea. I was the one who said you shouldn't do it. Well, maybe you'll get lucky and Mrs. Herrera will get fired soon." Rosie pulled a banana from her lunch bag and then put it back. "Oh, look, here comes Carson. Do you think he's brave enough to ask me to the dance? I wish Garrison would ask me. He's so mysterious, don't you think?"

Lila didn't think Carson was going to ask Rosie to the dance, though she would never say so. Carson might be cute, and he might be popular, but he was also strangely . . . decent. This morning he'd stood up in front of the class to announce that his mom had started making quilts for this cancer charity called Quilts for the Cure, and if anybody wanted to donate fabric or thread, that would be cool, but not to worry about it if they didn't. Practically all the girls in the class raised their hands and promised to bring in fabric the very next day. Carson looked like he might cry. Rosie had made fun of him later, but Lila thought it was nice he was trying to do something good. She wondered if his grandma had cancer.

"Okay, who's gonna friend me with a little math homework help?" Carson asked when he reached their table. He put his hands on the table and leaned in. "Lila? Give me some help and a smile-ah?"

"You're so dumb!" Rosie laughed, rolling her eyes. "It wasn't even hard homework!" She turned to Lila. "Maybe you ought to go look for that thing we were talking about? Like, now?"

Lila nodded mutely and slowly rose from her seat. She'd probably get in trouble for leaving the cafeteria before recess without permission, but did it really matter? She was in so much trouble already, and she didn't even know why. She never would have stolen anything from Mrs. Herrera if it weren't for Rosie acting like it was the big bonding thing they were doing together. "I'll be the lookout," Rosie had said on Monday morning, pushing Lila into the empty classroom. "We're partners in crime!"

"I don't know, Rosie," Lila had said, holding on to the doorframe. "This could be a really bad idea."

"What are you talking about? It's a great idea!" Rosie paused as she stepped back out into the hallway and looked left, then right. "We'll give it back after lunch. Or by tomorrow at the latest. Really, I just want to see if Mrs. Herrera even notices that it's gone."

"But what if something happens to it?" Lila said.

"Just go!" Rosie pushed Lila again, this time with a lot more force. "It's just a stupid photograph. What could happen to it? Now hurry up!"

It had only taken a couple of seconds to grab the picture of Mrs. Herrera's favorite teacher and shove it into her backpack, but that was enough time for Lila to wonder what she was doing and why she thought being friends with Rosie was a good idea. Oh, it had seemed like an awesome idea six weeks ago, when she'd been stuck with boring, geeky Ellie Barker. Rosie and Petra were much more her speed. They cared about clothes and being popular and having fun, everything that Lila cared about. They liked to talk about boys, Lila liked to talk about boys.

But then Petra had cut off her hair and Rosie acted like it was Lila's fault. She never did weird stuff like that before you started hanging out with us. It's like you threw her off balance, Rosie had texted her right after it happened. But how could Lila have thrown someone like Petra off balance? Petra wasn't a delicate flower that any wind could blow over. Petra was a humongous piece of granite that blocked your way. You couldn't get past her or knock her down. She was big and you were little, case closed.

Right before lunch Monday, Mrs. Herrera announced that several items had been taken from her special shelf, including her three ceramic kittens. Lila closed her eyes, trying to remember if the kittens had all been there when she'd stolen the photograph. But it had all happened so quickly—the mad dash into the classroom, the quick grab—that she hadn't had time to notice anything.

Had someone been in the room when she'd run in? Lila shivered. What if someone had been hiding in the book nook and had seen her?

She felt like everyone must be looking at her, but no, they were all looking at Becca and Henry, the obvious suspects. Who else would people think of before they thought of Lila? Maybe Petra? That gave Lila an idea. She leaned across the aisle toward Rosie and hissed, *"Petra,"* in her loudest whisper. Other kids heard her, and all of a sudden the echoes—*Petra, Petra, Petra*—bounced around the room.

So maybe nobody would ever point a finger at her. There was absolutely no reason to, not when there were so many other potential thieves in the classroom. And how likely was it that somebody had been hiding out in the book nook and had seen her? Not likely at all.

By the end of the day, Lila had almost forgotten that she was, in fact, a thief.

It wasn't until she got home Monday afternoon and

opened up her backpack that she remembered. But when she reached in to pull the photograph out (where would she hide it? And what would she say if her mom found it?), it was no longer there. Someone had taken it. Lila's entire body flooded with relief. How could she be caught if she didn't have stolen goods in her possession?

If only she didn't have to tell Rosie that it was gone.

But she knew there would be a price to pay if she didn't tell and Rosie found out later. There was always a price to pay with Rosie. If you said one wrong word— "guys" instead of "boys" (for some reason this was important to Rosie) or "stink" instead of "smells"—you paid for it for the rest of the day. Rosie's weapon was her phone; her ammunition was the group text.

When she finally confessed today that the picture was missing, Lila thought she'd feel better. *Just get out it out of your system,* she'd told herself on the way into the cafeteria. Maybe Rosie would just shrug and say, *Oh well, nothing we can do about it now.*

So why *hadn't* she said that? Lila wondered as she slunk along the hallway now in search of a photograph she was pretty sure she'd never find. Wasn't the problem out of their hands? They couldn't get caught because they didn't have the stolen object in their possession. Case closed.

She was nearing the library (maybe whoever had stolen the photograph out of Lila's backpack had stuck it behind some books?) when it dawned on her why Rosie wanted Lila to find it. If someone knew that Lila had it, they'd probably seen Lila steal it—and at the same time seen Rosie acting as lookout. But if Lila found the photograph and snuck it back onto Mrs. Herrera's special shelf, then she and Rosie could deny everything.

I am not going to cry, Lila insisted to herself, passing the library and heading to the computer lab instead. But she could feel the tears mounting an attack. If she wasn't careful, she'd be a blubbering mess in the middle of the hallway. She'd worked so hard this year not to cry! All summer she'd watched sad YouTube videos about lost kittens and small children in the hospital who need kidney transplants, pinching herself every time she felt the tears coming. Middle school was going to be different for Lila, she'd decided on the day they moved into the new house. No one was going to call her "crybaby" anymore or leave packs of tissue in her backpack with Post-it notes that read *Boo-hoo!* stuck to them. She was never going to be that girl again. Her parents' divorce was over and done with, she lived in a new town, was going to a new school. No one would ever know what a baby she'd been ever since third grade, when her mom and dad started fighting so much and everything had gotten terrible.

And she'd done it! She'd taught herself not to cry. And without even trying, she'd become one of the most popular girls in her class—the good kind of popular, as far as Lila was concerned, the kind where people didn't necessarily like you, but they wanted to be you. They were scared of you.

Lila liked people being scared of her. But they wouldn't be scared of her if they saw her running down the hallway with tears streaming down her face because she didn't know what to do and she really only had one friend and she pretty much hated that friend and she was pretty sure that friend hated her. . . .

A hard, firm voice inside her head ordered, *INTO THE BATHROOM, NOW!*

Lila sniffed hard and pushed her way into the girls' room. She would hide out until the tears passed out of her system. No one could see her cry. No one.

Not even that little mouse Aadita, who was standing at the sink washing her hands. Had Aadita been crying too? It sure looked like it, but Lila didn't care. "Get out of here!" she hissed. Aadita took a step back from the sink, but she didn't leave. She looked sad, but she didn't look scared.

Lila leaned in, trying to look menacing. "I said, get out of here, you jerk!"

Aadita flinched, but the only move she made was to pull a paper towel from the paper towel dispenser and dry her hands.

Lila couldn't stop herself. She grabbed Aadita by the arm and pulled her to the doorway. "Go cry somewhere else, crybaby! Why won't you leave?"

Aadita shook her head. Clearly she wasn't going to talk or leave. She was just going to stand there. Lila thought about pushing her out of the bathroom, but she'd never pushed anyone in her life, and besides, it was impossible to imagine pushing Aadita anywhere. It would be like trying to push a feather.

Lila knew what it was like to be a feather. She was the feather who got blown this way and that during the custody hearing, where a judge decided which parent she would live with and which one she'd see on weekends and holidays. She was the feather that twirled through the sky, round and round, not knowing where she would land.

She knew all about being a feather.

She opened her mouth to yell one more time, but her throat was filled with tears so all she could get out was, "Just go, okay? Please?"

Aadita nodded. She walked toward the door. But before she opened it, she turned to Lila and said, "I think you are nicer than you behave. I think you should find nicer friends."

It was the most words Lila had ever heard Aadita speak in a row. She didn't know what to say, and then there was nothing to say because Aadita was gone.

Lila sniffed. She sort of wished that Aadita would

come back, so they could talk some more. Did she really think Lila was nice? Lila didn't know if she was nicer than she acted or not. She just knew that being mean was safer. So after Aadita left, she blew her nose as hard as she could and splashed her face with water. She went into a stall and closed the door behind her so she could have a meditation moment before going back out into the hallway.

And if Aadita told anyone she'd found Lila crying in the bathroom, Lila would make her regret it.

Chapter Sixteen

Aadita

Wednesday, October 11

Aadita sat on her bed Wednesday night and studied the three tiny kittens in her hand. They were tiny, no bigger than grapes, and the one with the missing ear had the cutest expression, like it wanted nothing more than to rub against your arm and purr its heart out.

The kittens had been living with her since Monday, and Aadita had thought about naming them, but she knew they already had names given to them by Mrs. Herrera. Besides, they weren't hers and she had every intention of giving them back. But when? When it was safe, she supposed. When Lila had returned the photograph of Mrs. Herrera's favorite teacher and when the *Hatchet* thief placed the book back on the shelf that held Mrs. Herrera's special collection of special things. When everyone stopped being so strange.

"Aadita, how is your history project coming along? It is due next week, correct?"

Her father stood in the doorway. Aadita closed her hand over the kittens, although she knew her father wouldn't notice the tiny creatures, or have a second thought about them if he did.

"You look tired, Papa," she said. "You shouldn't travel so much."

Her father smiled. "It is part of my job, and besides, I get to travel to many wonderful places."

"Which you say you never really get to see."

"I see them on my way to and from the airport," her father said. "It's meeting the people I find interesting."

"You mean meeting transportation management geeks."

Her father smiled. "That is precisely what I mean. We get to talk about all the things that would bore our families to tears if we discussed them over the dinner table."

Aadita wished she could tell him about the kittens in her hand and ask for his advice, but she was afraid her father might not understand. He would be upset with her for stealing. But what she did on Monday morning really wasn't stealing, it was saving. Not that she expected anyone to know the difference.

It had been such a strange Monday from the very start. Normally Aadita's mother dropped her off at school at the usual time, but on this particular morning she had a dentist appointment, so she e-mailed Mrs. Herrera to see if Aadita could come to homeroom class twenty-five minutes early. Mrs. Herrera, it turned out, had a faculty meeting, but said she would leave the classroom unlocked for Aadita. Which was how Aadita came to be snuggled up in the book nook reading *The War That Saved My Life* when Lila and Rosie came to the door and started arguing about whether or not Lila should come in. "We're partners in crime," Rosie had said, and Aadita had shivered. What sort of awful thing were they about to do?

A few seconds later Lila (who clearly did not want to do this) raced into the room, grabbed the photograph from Mrs. Herrera's special shelf, and raced back out again.

"Here, you take it," Aadita could hear her saying to Rosie in the hallway, to which Rosie had responded, "No way! I'm not going to get caught with stolen goods."

Poor Lila, Aadita thought. She should have stayed friends with Ellie. Aadita would like to be friends with Ellie, but Ellie didn't seem to need any friends. She was so independent!

Aadita was about to sink back into the reading pillows when a sudden fear entered her. What if someone tried to steal Mrs. Herrera's kittens? She had to admit that if she was tempted by anything on Mrs. Herrera's special shelf for her special things, it was that tiny family of kittens, especially the one with only one ear. She would never steal them, of course, but what if someone else did? Her heart would break.

The idea to take the one-eared kitten into her protection was sudden and impossible to resist. Aadita had always had a fondness for broken things. Once, last year when she was shopping with her mother at Target, she asked her mother to buy a doll with a cracked face. Aadita didn't actually play with dolls anymore, and her mother rarely made impulse purchases, but she'd felt so sorry for that doll that surely no one would ever want or buy.

She looked up at the clock. She had five minutes before Mrs. Herrera was supposed to return from her meeting. It would only take her thirty seconds to grab the kitten, but then what would she do? Run away, like Lila and Rosie? But why? And besides, wouldn't Mrs. Herrera expect her to be there when she got back?

You are becoming overexcited, Aadita told herself. *Just take the kitten and put it in your backpack. When everything is over—when Lila returns the photograph and the danger is past—you will return the kitten to its home. Very simple.*

She walked over to the shelf as though she were only mildly interested in examining its contents. Should anyone come in, they wouldn't give her a second thought. She considered humming or whistling, but that would be overdoing it. No, she was just stretching a bit to wake up, taking a look at these half-interesting objects.

She glanced behind her, then snatched the little kitten, which she quickly deposited in her pocket. That was all she intended to take, but then the other two kittens looked up at her with such longing. . . .

She took a tissue from the box on Mrs. Herrera's desk and wrapped the three kittens in it before depositing them into the front pocket of her backpack. "Be safe," she whispered as she zipped up the pocket. "I will return you to your home soon."

Taking a deep breath, Aadita turned to go to her desk, only to find herself facing Sam Hawkins, who was staring at her from the doorway. Then, like a flash, he was gone, and Aadita wasn't sure whether she'd really seen him or just imagined it. If it really had been Sam, what was he doing back at school? More importantly, would he tell Mrs. Herrera that Aadita was a thief?

Moments later the others started trickling in—Cammi and Carson, Ben, Bart and Stefan, Henry—and Aadita felt her face flush. She'd never been guilty of a crime before! Did it show? Fortunately, no one looked at her at all except for Stefan, who smiled. Aadita smiled back and quickly opened her notebook so she wouldn't have to make eye contact with anyone else.

When Mrs. Herrera reported to the class that some of her things had been taken, Aadita tried to look as surprised as possible, doing her best not to glance in Lila's direction. Of course she was genuinely surprised when she learned that one of the items was *Hatchet*. And, oddly, she was relieved. Now she knew she'd made the right decision in rescuing the kittens. Clearly there were thieves all around her.

That afternoon she'd hidden the kittens away in her desk drawer. If her mother found them, Aadita would say they were a gift from Ariana.

By Wednesday, Aadita had begun to feel horribly guilty. Every day since Monday, Mrs. Herrera had locked her classroom during lunch and recess. She didn't trust the class anymore, and this made Aadita feel not only like she'd done something truly terrible, but like she'd done something harmful to others.

She was standing outside the classroom door after

recess, looking through the window and wondering whether Mrs. Herrera would let the class back in if she brought the kittens back, when Henry came up and tapped her on the shoulder.

Henry was always tapping her on the shoulder. Or bumping into her. Or lifting up a piece of her hair when he walked past her desk and saying, "Smooth!" or "Shiny!" Aadita tried not to mind. She thought it must be hard to be Henry, jumping around all the time, unable to keep himself under control.

"The classroom is locked," she said when he tapped her again.

"I don't want to go in," Henry replied. "I want to stay out. I wish we went to an outside school. We could put up tents when it started to rain."

Aadita giggled. Pokey-punchy Henry irritated her, but the Henry with the wild imagination didn't. She liked that Henry.

"So . . ." Henry took a step so he was standing beside her and they were both peering into Mrs. Herrera's dark classroom.

"Yes?" Aadita said.

"The dance? The Fall Ball? Would you do me the honor?"

Aadita looked at Henry, who was still looking through the window, but now his face was blushing a furious red. Henry wanted to go to the dance with her? How did that happen? Was it a joke?

"Are you pulling a prank on me, Henry?"

Henry shook his head. "This is not a prank or a joke or a trick. It is a question about whether or not you want to go to the Fall Ball. Very straightforward. Very no strings attached."

"I'm sorry, but I can't," Aadita said. She wanted to explain more, but somehow the words wouldn't come. It was always this way at school. At home she could talk and talk, but at school the words got swallowed up before she could say them.

"Henry," she tried, but still—nothing.

"Don't explain, don't explain!" Henry turned and exploded down the hall. "Stop talking! You can stop talking now."

Aadita opened her mouth to call after him. And still—nothing.

She had wanted to tell him she wasn't allowed to go to dances. Her mother had been very clear at the beginning of sixth grade. No dances, no boy-girl parties, no boyfriends. "I remember your sister's sixth-grade year very clearly," she'd said. "It all begins in sixth grade. All the romantic nonsense that you are far too young for."

Maybe she should write him a note. *Dear Henry, I didn't mean to hurt your feelings . . .*

But she had hurt his feelings! She'd hurt them very badly.

Aadita looked through the window into Mrs. Herrera's locked-up classroom and started to cry. It was unbearable to her that she had hurt Henry. That he thought she didn't like him. That he had been brave and asked her to the dance and she had had to say no.

The girls' room was just down the hall. When Aadita got there, she splashed water on her face. The bell was going to ring in five minutes, and she didn't want to go to math all red-eyed and weepy. But every time she thought of Henry's hurt expression and the fact that she would never be able to explain to him why she'd had to say no because every time she tried he would run away, the tears came back.

The door slammed open, and Lila—her fellow thief—stormed in. She looked like she was crying or was about to cry. But why? Was everyone crying today?

"Get out of here!" Lila yelled, and Aadita took a step back from the sink, not sure what to do. She couldn't go into the hallway looking like this, her face full of tears. Besides, who was Lila the thief to tell her to do anything?

Lila leaned in, making her face even meaner than before. "I said, get out of here, you jerk!"

Aadita flinched, but the only move she made was to pull a paper towel from the paper towel dispenser and dry her hands. Should she tell Lila she knew about the photograph? Should she confess her own crime as well?

Lila grabbed Aadita by the arm and dragged her to the doorway. "Go cry somewhere else, crybaby! Why won't you leave?"

Aadita pulled back her arm. What was wrong with everyone lately? Was the whole world going crazy? She felt sorry for Lila, she really did. Such a stupid choice to become friends with Rosie and Petra! She should say something to help Lila. She should reach out the hand of friendship, offer to go with Lila to Mrs. Herrera, where they could both admit to the terrible things they'd done. Then maybe all the tears would stop. Well, Aadita still had Henry to cry over. . . .

Her eyes filled with tears yet again. Perhaps she should go to the office and pretend to be ill.

Lila opened her mouth, like she had more yelling to do, but then she sighed loudly and said, "Just go, okay? Please?"

Aadita nodded. She walked toward the door. But before she opened it, she turned to Lila and said, "I think you are nicer than you behave. I think you should find nicer friends."

Lila stared at her. She opened her mouth and then closed it again. She looked sad.

Aadita decided it was just a very sad Wednesday, and there was nothing to be done about it except get through it. And try to avoid Henry, which was easy, because Henry was clearly trying to avoid her.

* * *

Her father was still standing in the doorway, looking at Aadita with a concerned expression. She wished she could tell him everything. She wished she could hand over all her problems to him like a basket of math equations for him to solve. Her father was very good at solving math equations.

But her father could not solve the problem of Henry's hurt feelings or do anything about the fact that Henry would never speak to her again or look at her or lift up a strand of her hair and say, "A bird's wing!" He couldn't solve the problem of when to return the three little kittens. He couldn't make Mrs. Herrera unlock her door during lunch and recess. He couldn't keep Mrs. Herrera from being in trouble with the vice principal for doing—well, whatever it was that Mrs. Herrera had done. Aadita didn't believe any of the rumors that she'd heard, but she worried nonetheless that one day she would arrive to school to find another teacher in Mrs. Herrera's place.

Aadita wasn't sure if she liked sixth grade, not if sixth grade was a place where her father could no longer sit on the edge of her bed and tell her how to solve her problems the way he'd always been able to before.

"Don't look so sad, Papa!" Aadita said, trying not to feel so sad herself. She crossed the room to give her father a hug. "My project is almost done and everything is good!"

Her father rubbed the top of her head. "If you are sure . . ."

"I'm sure, Papa," Aadita insisted, although she was only sure of one thing, and that was that somehow, some way, she had to give the kittens back.

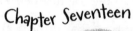

Chapter Seventeen

Matt

Thursday, October 12

Teachers thought after-school detention was the worst thing they could do to you, and, okay, yeah, Matt had to admit as he stood in the doorway and looked around Mr. Woodcroft's room, it was pretty boring. But the worst thing was going home and having to deal with Parker, who was back from rehab and making everybody miserable. He acted like he was king of the universe, the way he ordered them all around—"Matt, go get me a Coke! Hey, Mom, I need a snack!"—and he made you feel like if you didn't do what he said, he'd start doing all that stuff again that got him into rehab in the first place.

So, yeah, compared to spending the rest of his day being treated like somebody's servant, after-school detention wasn't that bad. It was kind of entertaining, if you looked at it the right way. Who would join him today? Would it be the regulars, or would someone new pop in who you never expected to see? And what kind of mood would Mr. Woodcroft be in? Some days he was total Mr. Laid-Back, all *Do what you want, just keep it to a dull roar,* and other days he was Mr. Dictator, walking up and down the aisles and checking to make sure you were doing homework, or at the very least reading a magazine.

Today appeared to be a Mr. Laid-Back day. When Matt walked into the room, Mr. Woodcroft was at his desk, feet up, reading this week's *Sports Illustrated.* Good. That meant if things got really boring, Matt could yell out, "Hey, Mr. W, did you know the Bengals suck?" and they could spend the whole time talking about football.

He eyeballed the rows of desks to see who was here. Kurt Wells, one of the regulars, along with Russ Meacham and Cody Milne. Jenna Figge was in her usual seat (last row, far left desk), and Stasia Lowe was hunkered over a magazine three desks up and one desk over. Looked like it was the usual crew today.

But wait! Whoa ho! Who was that in the desk by the back window? Could it be Milton Falls Middle School's newest basket case, Becca Hobbes? Oh, this was too good, Matt thought. This would make after-school detention fly by.

"Becca, Becca, Becca," he whispered to everybody's favorite former good girl as he sat down in the desk behind her. "What are you in for? Murder? Theft? A little shoplifting from the school store, maybe?"

Becca didn't turn around. For a minute Matt thought she wasn't going to respond at all, but then she said, "I'm a volunteer."

"You're a what?"

"A volunteer," Becca repeated, still looking straight ahead. "I thought I'd see what it was like here."

Matt laughed. Man, this girl was strange. "So you're saying you didn't actually do anything wrong, you just decided to spend your afternoon in detention?"

"Yes, that's exactly what I'm saying."

"Wow, you're even nuttier than I thought."

Becca's shoulders stiffened, but she didn't reply.

"Mr. Collins, I'd like to see some homework on your desk," Mr. Woodcroft said in a tone of voice that Matt interpreted as meaning *If you don't bother me, I won't bother you. Let's just make this look legit.*

"Sure, Mr. Woodcroft," Matt replied cheerfully. "Getting it out right now."

He reached into his backpack and pulled out a pencil and a notebook. Since he had no intention of doing homework (he'd very politely ask Bart if he could copy his on the bus in the morning—Bart never said no), it didn't matter which notebook he got out. In this case, it turned out to be history. Oh, man, the stupid history project on democracy in ancient Greece—when was that due? Tomorrow? Monday?

He poked Becca with his pencil. "When's that history project due?"

"Monday," Becca whispered. "But Mrs. Hulka wants a bibliography of all your sources by tomorrow."

"Sources? What?"

Becca finally turned around. "A list of the books

you read and any Internet sites you got information from? It's all on the sheet she gave us."

Matt looked in his notebook. No sheets, no nothing. "I think I lost it. Can I see yours?"

"Have you even started on this project?" Becca sounded annoyed. "Checked out one book from the library?"

"Uh, no?" Matt said with a shrug and a smile. "It's not due until Monday, right?"

"It's thirty percent of your grade for this quarter!"

"So what? I'll do it over the weekend."

Becca turned back around. What was up with this girl? Matt wondered. For years she'd been the world's biggest goody-goody, and now she'd decided she was some juvenile delinquent, but she still cared about history projects? Matt had seen her eating by herself in the cafeteria when she used to eat with Cammi all the time (Cammi, Carson's new best buddy—how bizarre was that?) and was in everybody's business. Now she was this dark loner or something. Pretty soon she'd be like Parker's old girlfriend, the one who wore a dog collar and shaved her head.

He poked Becca with his pencil again. "Listen, I could use your help," he said, although he really didn't care about the history project. He could pull some stuff off the Internet and turn it in on Monday, complete with pictures. He did it all the time. But he was interested in this new Becca. What was her deal?

"Leave me alone," Becca whispered, even though nobody else was whispering. *See,* Matt wanted to tell someone, *once a goody-goody, always a goody-goody.*

"You're smart, everybody knows that. You're probably the second-smartest person in Mrs. Herrera's homeroom, after Ben."

"And Stefan," Becca pointed out. She turned around and looked at Matt again. "Although I actually got a better grade on the last science quiz."

"So you're still studying and everything?" Matt asked. "Even though you've kind of—kind of gone bad? I mean, what happened in the art room with you and Petra anyway? How'd you end up cutting off your hair and everything?"

Becca's face went red. "It was stupid. She tricked me into thinking we were friends."

Then she started to cry, and Matt wished he'd never started this conversation. He was so over people crying. His mom had spent the last year and a half crying about Parker and all his problems. At first Matt had tried being nice to her and telling her she shouldn't worry so much, but she'd just wave him off, like he didn't know what he was talking about. Which was when he had figured out that the only kid who mattered at his house was Parker. Forget Matt, forget his sister, Holly. It was Parker 24/7.

"Stop, okay?" Matt said, trying to shake Becca out of feeling sorry for herself. "You're acting like you're the first one Petra ever used. But really the joke's on her, right? She's the one who came out looking like a loser."

"Yeah, but she *wanted* to look like a loser," Becca said, sniffling. "You know what she said to me?"

Matt couldn't wait to hear this. "What?"

"That she was bored to death of being Petra Wilde and was ready to be somebody else for a change."

"Okay, so that's different," Matt said. Why wouldn't anybody want to be Petra? She ruled their grade. She could make anybody do anything she wanted to. She'd made Becca, the girl who never broke a rule in her life, cut off her hair and trash the art room. Who would give up that kind of power voluntarily?

"So how'd she talk you into it anyway?" Matt asked. "I mean, the haircut and all."

Becca gave him a strange look and shrugged. "She didn't really have to talk me into it. I just wanted to do something—different, I guess. I was tired of the old Becca Hobbes." Her eyes welled with tears again. "Except now I sort of miss her!"

"Who?" Matt asked, confused. "Petra?"

"No!" Becca practically shouted, but she turned the volume back down to a whisper before Mr. Woodcroft could say anything. "The old me. But it's too late to turn back now. Besides, what's the use? Cammi's not my friend anymore, and I'm never going to be Mrs. Herrera's favorite, so why try?"

Matt was definitely having a hard time keeping up. "Why try what?"

"Do you know how hard I worked to make Mrs. Herrera like me?" Becca practically hissed. "I did everything I could!"

Okay, now Matt was totally lost. "What does that have to do with cutting off your hair?"

Becca shook her head. "Forget it. You wouldn't understand. I mean I just wanted her to like me."

"Who? Petra?"

"Mrs. Herrera!"

"Who says Mrs. Herrera doesn't like you?"

Becca glared at met. "She didn't eat the Oreos I gave her!"

Wow, this girl was a nutjob! Still, Matt felt kind of sorry for her. If he understood what she was saying, Becca had tried her usual brownnosing routine with Mrs. Herrera, but Mrs. Herrera didn't take the bait. Which on the one hand was cool. It meant that Mrs. Herrera didn't play favorites. But on the other hand, he could see why it bummed Becca out. Brownnosing had always worked for her before. Now what was she supposed to do?

"You ever try talking to her?"

"Who? Petra?"

Matt sighed. "No, Mrs. Herrera. Maybe she's allergic to Oreos. Maybe she was saving them for a special treat. Like a reward or something. My brother Parker?

He's on this whole reward system. So, say he doesn't skip any classes for a week, my mom gets him Chick-fil-A for dinner on Friday night. Maybe Mrs. Herrera was saving the Oreos for when she did something good."

Becca's eyes widened. Matt could tell that thought had never crossed her mind. "Do you think that's it?"

"Could be," Matt said with a shrug. "It sounds like she's got some bad habits, right, or why else is she in such big trouble with the veep?"

"The veep?"

"The vice principal," Matt explained patiently. "'You're on thin ice, Judith'—remember? So maybe Mrs. Herrera's on thin ice because she got caught drinking beer in the teachers' lounge. Maybe she's saving those Oreos to celebrate thirty days of sobriety. You could always ask her why they're still in her desk. But are those Oreos really the reason you're all different now? I mean, you're mad at Mrs. Herrera, so now you're going to be this bad person?"

Becca leaned her head close to Matt's. "Can I tell you something? That you promise not tell anyone else?"

Matt nodded.

"I hate being bad. I'm really terrible at it!"

Matt wanted to roll on the floor laughing. The idea that Becca was bad because she'd cut off her hair and had checked herself voluntarily into detention? Hilarious! What an amateur. She had no idea what bad was.

But he kept it under control; otherwise she might start crying again. "Maybe you ought to shoot for medium. Not bad, but not so good all the time. Like, don't try to be good just to make people like you?"

Becca seemed to think this over. "Maybe," she said, sounding doubtful. "But I like being good."

"That's funny, because I like being bad," Matt said with a grin.

"So maybe *you* should shoot for medium," Becca said.

"Nah," Matt said, poking Becca's arm with his pencil. "I've got a reputation to protect."

Becca turned back around and picked up her backpack. Was she going to head out, since she wasn't supposed to be here in the first place? Would Matt head out if he was free to go?

Free to go where, that was the question. Home? He'd rather be here.

"Okay, you can borrow this if you want," Becca said, shoving a piece a paper at him. "It's the requirements for the project. And if you want, I bet Mr. Woodcroft would let you go to the library with me and I can show you some books you could use for your bibliography."

"I think Mrs. Rosen banned me from the library," Matt said.

Becca rolled her eyes. "She won't ban you if you're with me. Unlike some other people I could name, Mrs. Rosen appreciates the Oreos I give her."

"Okay, I guess," Matt said, thinking it might be nice to have a change of scenery. "If it's okay with Mr. Woodcroft."

"Wait here," Becca said, zipping up her backpack. Two seconds later she was up at Mr. Woodcroft's desk, and two seconds after that she was waving to Matt to follow her.

"Teachers just do what you say, don't they?" Matt said as they walked out into the hallway.

"Most teachers," Becca replied. "The ones who know what's good for them."

Matt snorted. Maybe Becca was more interesting than he'd given her credit for. Which reminded him. "Hey, Becca, there's something I've been wondering. Are you the one who stole Mrs. Herrera's stuff?"

"Wouldn't you like to know?" Becca said, raising her left eyebrow like she was this mysterious person or something. "Okay, now if you're going to do this project right, you've got to do three things. . . ."

Matt followed Becca up the hallway to the library, tuning out her instructions. The fact was, he was kind of getting a kick out of Becca Hobbes, even if she was the world's biggest pain in the butt. Maybe he could help her get back on the straight-and-narrow path. He didn't mind the idea of helping some loser out every once in a while, though he didn't plan on making it a habit. Making people miserable was too much fun—in fact, it was what Matt Collins was all about.

Chapter Eighteen

Bart

Thursday, October 12

As soon as Bart saw Matt Collins get on the bus, he went into lockdown. *Remember the rules,* he told himself: no eye contact, no sudden movements. Don't pretend to be enjoying the view through the window; for some reason that seemed to be a red flag for Matt, a sign that Bart might be experiencing some happiness at the moment and needed to be brought back down to earth. Ditto for reading. However, looking depressed was also inadvisable, as it brought out Matt's *I'll give you something to cry about* side.

The trick was to look straight ahead without

appearing to actually be looking at anything in particular. Unfocus the eyes, relax the facial muscles. You
can't appear to be thinking about anything, processing
information, or showing interest in your surroundings
in any way. You must be a blank page.

With any luck, someone will sit next to you before
Matt gets a chance. Do not acknowledge this person
in any way unless you have to. More likely than not,
the person taking the seat will not acknowledge you,
either, so this is typically not a problem. Think of this
person as a cushion or a kind of life preserver. Pray
that you get off the bus before he or she does.

If Bart followed every rule to perfection, he might—
just might—have a nice ride home. He'd stayed after
school today to work with Stefan and Ben on the computer game they were developing, the one that was
going to make them all rich. Bart was in charge of the
game narrative, and he liked looking out the bus window and thinking up new twists and turns that the
plot could take, creating new quests, coming up with
new monsters. He wished he could spend all day in the
computer lab working on this stuff.

It wasn't that he hated school—he liked his teachers a lot, and he really liked history this year—he just hated being *at* school, at least when he wasn't in the lab. School was where he got teased and pushed and laughed at. Home was where he could be himself and nobody thought he was strange or goofy. At home, he was incredibly popular, even if he did bite his nails and had early-onset acne. He was liked not only by his parents, Jim and Reesa, but also by his brother, Carl, a ninth grader with the same social skills set as Bart, meaning zero. But at home the lack of social skills didn't matter. Actually, at home Bart and Carl were both socially gifted. They were funny and entertaining and great conversationalists. But when Bart brought these gifts to school, they didn't have the same effect on people. Well, Ben and Stefan mostly got his jokes and they didn't seem to mind him hanging around, but everyone else treated Bart like a disease they were afraid of catching.

Except for Matt Collins on the bus ride home.

Before anyone else could join him, Matt plopped down next to Bart. A sharp elbow landed in Bart's side.

"You think I'm going to ask you for the history homework, don't you?" Matt asked gleefully. "You think I'm going to say, 'About that project that's due on Monday, I'll need you to do it for me,' am I right?"

Actually, Bart hadn't been thinking that. Matt often asked to copy his homework, but a project was a different thing. You couldn't just copy somebody's project and expect to get away with it, he wanted to tell Matt. But of course he didn't tell Matt anything, because he was hoping to make it home alive.

"Well, you're wrong, Mr. Nubby Nails," Matt went on. "I've got sources and an outline. What do you think about that?"

This was where things got dangerous. To reply or not to reply? Bart decided to risk it. "That's, uh, good?"

"Yeah, bro! Did you think it was bad? Quit being such a wuss-wad. And get this—Becca is coming over to my house on Sunday to help me with the finished product. I'm going to write a first draft tomorrow."

Bart couldn't help it. Breaking one of his most basic rules, he looked directly at Matt. "You've already started your project? And Becca is helping you? Why?"

"She likes me, dweeb-mush. Besides, I'm helping her out with something. It's kind of a trade."

Better not reply, you've said too much already, Bart told himself. He faced front again.

Matt elbowed him, this time with the potential for bruising. "Come on, bro. I expect to see a little more excitement from you!"

Bart sighed. He could see he had no choice but to engage. "That's great about the project. And I'm glad you and Becca are friends. She could use a friend right now."

"Now, don't get carried away, Bart the Fart," Matt said. "I didn't say we were friends. We're more like—I don't know, colleagues."

"That's good," Bart said before he could stop himself. "I mean, Becca's been so strange lately. I've been worried about her."

Bart, you idiot! What are you thinking? He braced himself for some rib crushing in the guise of a playful punch, but after a second he realized that Matt didn't seem to be angry. Still, Bart didn't relax. Relaxing was dangerous.

"Yeah, she's been acting pretty strange," Matt agreed. "Like that stuff with Petra. It's pretty bizzaro, bro. I mean, you know Becca. She's the last person in the world to break bad."

Bart nodded. He did know Becca. He'd known her since preschool. Not only had Becca never been a rule breaker, she'd actually been a lot like the secret police, tattling on people for the most minor infractions. This new side of Becca had been upsetting to Bart. How did you become a totally different person overnight? It was as if aliens had taken over Becca's body.

Matt slid down in the seat a little, like he was starting to get comfortable. "A lot of people think she stole Mrs. Herrera's stuff, did you know that? And I get it, I guess. You wouldn't have believed it two weeks ago, but now you'd believe anything about Becca. Except I know she's not like that. Between you and me, she doesn't like this new person she's become. It's a bad fit, am I right?"

Bart had to admit that Matt was right. Becca Hobbes was not a convincing bad girl. "It kind of makes me sad," he said, which he knew sounded goofy, but it was true. "I never thought she wanted to be bad."

"Exactly," Matt said, nodding. "And I agree, bro, it *is* sad."

They sat in a comfortable silence for a minute, until Bart asked, "What happened, do you know? Because it happened all of a sudden." He snapped his fingers. "Just like that."

Matt lowered his voice to a whisper. "Dude, Mrs. Herrera doesn't like her. Or at least that's what Becca thinks. So her feelings are hurt..."

"And she's acting out," Bart finished for him.

"Exactly."

Bart leaned back and pondered his next move. Keep the conversation going? He could mention what he'd heard about Mrs. Herrera's "thin ice" problem, which wasn't that big of a deal. In fact, it was sort of disappointing. Henry had told Stefan (and Stefan had told Bart and Ben) that last year Mrs. Herrera had given some student permission to take a day off school so she could do some research at the zoo. The girl's mom had gone too, so you think that it would have been okay, but apparently it wasn't, not unless your teacher filled out two tons of paperwork explaining why you should be excused, which Mrs. Herrera hadn't. Apparently a teacher couldn't just give a kid a day off, even to work on a big project.

Matt elbowed Bart in the side again. "Dude, why so quiet?"

"Uh, I was just thinking about Becca," Bart lied, deciding he didn't want to tell Matt Henry's story; Matt wouldn't believe him anyway. "So if Becca didn't steal Mrs. Herrera's things, then who did?" he asked, deciding to stay on what seemed to be safe territory. "I know some people say it's Petra, but I don't know."

"Maybe Petra," Matt replied. "Or maybe that new girl. Ellie? Who knows what she's capable of?"

Bart didn't think it was Ellie, but why introduce conflict into what was turning into a pleasant conversation? "I guess it could be her. Or Henry."

"Yeah, it's probably Henry," Matt agreed. "Only if it was Henry, don't you think he would have blabbed it all over the place by now?"

"Probably. So maybe Ellie, or maybe . . ." Bart paused. Should he make a joke? They were pretty close to his stop, so why not? He was almost home free. "Maybe Aadita?"

Matt slapped Bart on the knee, which hurt but didn't seem to be intended to injure. "Yeah, bro, Aadita! Hide your wallets, guys! Here comes Aadita!"

Bart laughed, but then he worried that Matt would start repeating the joke to everybody he knew and might start teasing Aadita while he was at it. "I guess we shouldn't joke about it, though, right? I wouldn't want it to get back to Aadita—she might not know we were kidding."

Matt stopped laughing. He sat back up straight. "You were the one who made the joke, Bart the Fart."

Bart held up his hands in surrender. "I know, I know. Totally my bad. I'm just saying—"

"For a second there, I thought you were halfway cool," Matt said, shaking his head sadly. "Dude, you disappoint me."

"Sorry," Bart said, his voice barely rising above a whisper. "I just don't . . . well, um, here's my stop. Good luck with the project."

Matt didn't move, so Bart had to climb over him to

get out of the seat. Just as he was stepping into the aisle, Matt leaned into him so that he went sprawling toward the front, falling the last few feet to the steps.

"You are off my bus until further notice!" Mr. Simms, the bus driver, yelled. "I can't put up with these kinds of shenanigans."

"But—but—" Bart started to protest as he rose to his feet.

"Why don't you wipe your butt sometime, butt-wad?" Matt called, and everyone on the bus cracked up. "Maybe then you wouldn't stink so bad."

Bart sighed. He turned to Mr. Simms. "You can't kick me off the bus for tripping. I know my rights."

"Get off now!" Mr. Simms commanded, waving dramatically toward the open door.

Bart got off. After the bus pulled away from the curb, he looked down at his knees. Only one of them was bleeding, so that was good. And it really didn't hurt that bad. Probably tonight it would stiffen up a little, but his mom had this cool little pillow filled with rice that you could microwave and put on sore muscles to make them loosen up.

He began limping home, and by the time he reached his driveway, his limp was barely there and his knee had pretty much stopped bleeding. Good as new, he thought as reached his front door. Maybe even better.

Chapter Nineteen

Ellie

Monday, October 16

After Mrs. Herrera took roll on Monday morning, she stood in front of the class and said, "I have an announcement to make."

Ellie sat up straight in her seat. Had the missing things been returned? Had more things been stolen? A cloud of whispers rose up behind her, and she knew everyone else was wondering the same thing.

"Actually, I have several announcements," Mrs. Herrera continued. "First, it appears Petra is switching schools. She was on the waiting list for the Lakewood Friends School and there was an unexpected opening last week."

Surprisingly, Ellie observed, a lot of people looked sad, people you never would have expected, like Rogan and Ben and Stefan. And Rosie looked like she might cry! Didn't Rosie hate Petra now? Didn't she think Petra was an untouchable?

Matt looked bummed. Garrison looked indifferent, like he couldn't be bothered to care (which was how Garrison always looked). Ariana had an *I told you so* expression on her face, as though she could have predicted Petra Wilde wasn't long for their classroom after her disastrous haircut.

"Next," Mrs. Herrera said, "I want to tell you is that my missing kittens have been returned, along with a very nice note of apology. I now understand why they were taken, and I'm not angry. I would very much like my copy of *Hatchet* back and most of all the photograph of my teacher, Mrs. Abbott. She died last year, so it makes me especially sad that my only picture of her is missing. If you took either of these things and would like to return them, leave them in a large envelope with my name on it in the front office. Write me a note and explain why you took it—or them—and all will be forgiven."

The loudspeaker over the classroom door buzzed to life. "Good morning, students!" a tinny voice greeted them. "Have you bought your tickets to the Fall Ball yet? You'll have a ball if you go, so don't delay! Today's lunch menu has the following delicious items. . . ."

The kittens had been returned! Wasn't Mrs. Herrera going to tell the class who took them and why? Ellie guessed probably not. She felt like there were all kinds of things Mrs. Herrera was never going to tell them, like why she was on thin ice, for instance. Or why she was letting Sam Hawkins hang out in her classroom when no one else was around. Ellie had been looking for clues for a week now, watching and listening—okay, okay, spying—and she could conclude only one thing: Sam Hawkins was coming back to his old school on a nearly daily basis.

And she was pretty sure he'd stolen her notebook last Tuesday.

Ellie had looked for her notebook everywhere. Her backpack, her locker, homeroom, Mrs. Hulka's room, the school's lost and found.

"Just ask around," her mother had said when she

found Ellie tearing through her backpack for the third time the day it disappeared. "Someone probably accidentally picked it up."

That was what Ellie had worried about—that someone had accidentally (or on purpose) taken her notebook and was deciding what to do with it. If they shared what she'd written about her various classmates, Ellie would be done for. It wasn't that she'd written anything mean; she'd just tried to write the truth. But who wanted to hear the truth about themselves, or at least another person's version of the truth? Did Bart want to be reminded that he bit his fingernails during tests and quizzes? How would Ariana feel when she learned at least one observer thought that deep down, there was a little meanness mixed in with all that niceness?

She had no idea why this stuff would be interesting to Sam, now that he wasn't in their class anymore. But maybe Sam was a writer, same as her, and writers made a point of being interested in everything.

Ellie glanced at the clock. They had five minutes before the bell rang for first period. She pulled out her new notebook and wrote, *Petra Wilde is gone for good.*

Who will she be at her new school? Will she go back to act-ing like old, mean Petra? Or will she continue down this new path? What if she's the one who stole Mrs. Herrera's kittens and returned them before she left?

Ellie sat up and chewed on her pen. But why would Petra have stolen the kittens in the first place? Even with her new hair, she wasn't really the tiny ceramic kitten type. Maybe it was Becca Hobbes after all. She'd seen Becca on Friday tidying up the book nook just like it was old times, like the haircutting incident had never happened. And she'd seen her helping Matt Collins with his history project on Friday in Mrs. Hulka's class. Matt had been really vocal about it too. "Gee, Becca! Thanks for your help! Wish everyone was as helpful as you are!" Weird. It was like Matt had become her press agent.

So the old, goody-goody Becca Hobbes was back. Maybe bad Becca had stolen the kittens and the newly good Becca had returned them. Ellie wrote this down. It was a theory worth pursuing.

"Ellie?"

Ellie looked up to see Felicity Wallack standing next

to her desk. Had she been reading over Ellie's shoulder? Ellie leaned over her notebook and covered it with her arm. "Uh, hi," she said. "What's up?"

Felicity shrugged. "Nothing. What are you writing? Not that it's any of my business. I'm just being nosy."

Ellie had been writing in one notebook or another since the beginning of school, and Felicity was the first person to ever ask what she was writing about. Not that Ellie wanted to admit she'd been taking notes on her classmates. "Just a story about a kid who's hiding out in his old school," she halfway lied. True, she was working on a story like that, just not at this very second.

Felicity's eyes widened. She leaned down close to Ellie. "So you've seen him too? Sam, I mean?"

"A lot of people have," Ellie replied. "Have you?"

"I saw him outside this morning," Felicity said in a quiet voice. "I was looking for my spelling notebook before school—I thought maybe I left it on the playground on Friday—and he poked his head around the corner of the building. You know where Becca used to hang out at recess? That's where he was."

"This morning?"

Felicity nodded. "And Henry told me he saw him in the bathroom last week."

"I've seen him a couple of times," Ellie said, deciding not to mention that one of those times had been in the middle of the school day, in this very classroom.

"You know what the funny thing is?" Felicity leaned even closer to Ellie and lowered her voice to a whisper. "Elizabeth said that she and Petra saw him at the homeless shelter on Saturday, when they took over some clothes to donate."

What was Sam Hawkins doing at the homeless shelter? Was it near his new neighborhood?

"Something strange is going on," Ellie said. "Something really strange and mysterious."

Felicity nodded. "I think so too. Do you think Mrs. Herrera knows about it?"

Oh, Mrs. Herrera knew about it, all right—whatever *it* was, Ellie thought. She had to. But for some reason, Ellie was reluctant to share this information with Felicity. Felicity hadn't really been a part of their class. Maybe she'd use the fact that Sam had been seen in Mrs. Herrera's classroom during the school day against their teacher, who as everyone knew, was already in some kind of trouble.

"What do *you* think?" Ellie asked, avoiding the question herself.

"I don't know," Felicity admitted. "I mean, why would she?"

"Almost time for the bell," Mrs. Herrera called out. "Start gathering your things."

Felicity stood up. She looked uncomfortable. "Listen," she said, "I think I have something that's yours? Someone gave it to me in car pool last week, only I'm not supposed to say who."

She went back to her desk and returned a moment later with Ellie's missing notebook, which Ellie snatched out of her hands, holding it tightly to her chest. "Last week? You've had this since last week? Did you read it?"

Felicity nodded, turning red. "The person who gave it to me to give you told me not to, but I couldn't help it. Actually, I learned a lot. I mean, you're really observant."

Not about you, Ellie almost said, and it was almost like Felicity had read her mind. "Not that there's much about me in there," she said. "I guess in a way I haven't really been a part of this class."

"Not really," Ellie agreed. "I mean, you're in classes with us and everything. Your brain is in this class. Your heart is with Mr. Lee's class."

Felicity's expression darkened. "Maybe not so much anymore."

"Oh," Ellie said. Her fingers itched to start taking notes. At last she was getting the inside scoop on Felicity Wallack!

And then she remembered Felicity had read her scoop on everybody else.

"Are you going to tell everybody what I wrote about them?" Ellie asked. "It probably doesn't matter, but I guess I don't want everyone to hate me. Even though they sort of do already."

Felicity was opening her mouth to say something when the bell rang. *Oh well,* Ellie thought as she stuffed her notebook into her backpack. It wasn't like she could lose any friends, since she didn't have any to begin with.

"Do you want to sit together at lunch today?" Felicity

asked as Ellie was starting to stand up, which made Ellie sit right back down.

"You mean together?"

Felicity nodded. "I'm pretty sure that's what I just said. I mean, we've eaten lunch apart up to now, right?"

"I'll eat lunch with you," Ellie said, trying to keep the excitement out of her voice. "I mean, if you really want to."

"Good," Felicity said. "I'd love to figure out this deal with Sam, what's going on. Do you think he's in trouble? Maybe he's why Mrs. Herrera is on thin ice. I wonder if there's something we can do to help him—and Mrs. Herrera. And who do you think took the kittens? Was it the same person who returned them?"

Felicity kept talking as Ellie got up and followed her to her desk. Who knew she was this chatty? Or this curious?

It was the third week of October, nearly two months into sixth grade, and Ellie Barker was pretty sure she was about to make her first friend.

Chapter Twenty

Garrison

Tuesday, October 17

Dear Mrs. Herrera,

I have a confession to make.

I'm not who you think I am.

Okay, maybe in some ways I really am who you think I am. You think I'm a jock, and I am a jock. I play AAU football in the fall and travel lacrosse in the spring. Football's my number one sport, but I have to give it up in ninth grade. My dad played college ball and even went to the NFL's Combine in February of his senior year. But he didn't get drafted, so he let football go and went back to school to get a business degree. Now he's glad he did, because a bunch of his buddies who played in the NFL are starting to have some serious health problems from too many concussions and injuries. That's why I can't play in high school, even though the rules are changing and the safety equipment's a lot better now.

There's things about being a jock that I like, and some things that I don't. The most obvious is that I like playing sports. I like the way I'm tired in a really good way at the end of the day. I feel used up, like I put everything I had out there. That's what my lacrosse coach says, leave it all on the field, don't save anything for later.

What don't I like? Getting automatically lumped in with a group of people, like everyone who's an athlete is exactly the same. It wasn't like that in elementary school. I mean, there were some people who were good at sports, like me and Carson, and some people who stunk up the gym, like Stefan and Bart, but being good at sports was just one part of who you were. Just one part of who people thought you were. And I had friends who weren't into sports, like Jason Donnell, who's in Mrs. Logan's homeroom this year, and nobody acted like we shouldn't be friends because I played sports and he didn't, except for swimming.

Last year nobody called me a jock, and this year everybody does. I'm in a category now, so people think they know all about me. They think I think I'm cool (I'm not), and they think I'm probably dumb (even though I'm in pre-algebra with Stefan and Ben), and they think every girl's in love with me and that I'm into all the hot girls. Girls keeping texting me and asking me who I like and who I think is hot and who I'm taking to the dance. One girl texted me a selfie with her tongue sticking out. I think she was trying to be sexy or something, but it was sort of gross. My mom checks my texts, and when she saw that one, she was totally freaked out. She called the girl's mom, and the girl's mom yelled at my mom. She said that boys like me force girls to act that way.

I don't even know what she was talking about.

I don't even like girls. I mean, not like that. Not yet anyway. But everyone thinks that I do or I should or that I should be all happy because a girl wants to text me a picture of her tongue hanging out.

You might think I'm the kind of guy who likes sitting at a crowded cafeteria table with all the other jocks and girls like the tongue-texting girl, but I don't. I mean, yeah, I sit at that table, mostly because I don't know where else to sit. That's where people expect me to sit. One time I tried sitting with Ethan, Rogan, and Cole, but they acted all goofy, even though Ethan and I went to the same lacrosse camp this summer and played on the same team in fourth grade.

The good thing that happened that day? Ethan was talking about this book you gave him called *Hatchet* and how it was the most awesome book ever. The more he talked about it, the more I wanted to read it. The more he talked about it, the more I wanted to be Brian, a kid stranded on a desert island with only his wits and a hatchet to survive. That sounded like the coolest thing ever.

I went to the library, but *Hatchet* was checked out. Ethan had the copy from the book nook. That only left one copy. Your copy.

I took it on Friday afternoon, thinking that I'd bring it back Monday morning and you'd never know it was gone. It didn't even feel like stealing to me. It just felt like borrowing without permission. I'm pretty sure there's a difference. Besides, I felt like I had to read that book right away. It's like I needed it to survive.

Remember the girl who sent me that text? The night before I stole *Hatchet*, she sent me another one. It was a picture of her in her nightgown. It wasn't like she was showing anything, but it wasn't supposed to be this innocent picture, either. I deleted it before my mom could see it, and I blocked her, but it bugged me even more than the first one. Why did she keep sending me this stuff? Did she think I liked it? Did she think I liked her? Why would she think that? I'd never even spoken to her.

I know I'm supposed to like getting those

texts. You probably think I do. But I don't. So when Ethan was talking about this kid getting stranded on an island in the middle of nowhere, I was like, Dude, take me there now. Seriously. Because I'd rather be roughing it on a deserted island than dealing with that girl and her crap.

I don't have to tell you that it's an awesome book. You might not think I'd be into camping or fishing or survival stuff like that, but I totally am. My dad's big on camping, so he takes me and my little sister Florence on camping trips in the fall, after football season's over. My mom stays home because she refuses to sleep on the ground.

You might not think I'm the kind of person who would read the same book three times in one weekend, but I am. It helped that my game got rained out Saturday and I didn't have a lot of homework. And it helped that I could totally see myself in Brian's shoes, except for the part about wanting to be rescued. Me, I'd rather be left alone for a while. I mean I know I'd get lonely. I'd miss my family and I'd miss playing football. But sometimes being alone just seems easier. Nobody's saying, *You're supposed to be this way* or *You're supposed to be that way.* You can just be who you are, no comment.

Anyway, I meant to give *Hatchet* back on that Monday, but I left it at home by accident. I left it home by accident for a week. My mom says that sometimes I do things accidentally on purpose. To be honest, I might not have ever brought it back, but yesterday I heard about how you're probably going to get fired because you're letting some homeless kid hang out in your classroom. I hope that doesn't happen, but if it does, I think you should read this book again.

I think you might need *Hatchet* more than I do right now.

Your student,

Garrison

PS I heard the homeless kid is Sam. Is that true?

Chapter Twenty-One

Cole

Wednesday, October 18

Cole sat at one end of the two cafeteria tables they'd pushed together and checked to see if all the members of the class were here. Where was Stefan? Oh, okay, there he was, crammed between Carson and Ben. Ben was next to Bart and Bart was next to Ellie, who was next to Rogan who was next to Ariana who was across from Elizabeth and so on and so on. Everybody was present and accounted for, except for Petra (who was no longer a member of the class), Rosie, and Lila. Rosie, had sneered at the very idea of a class meeting.

"Why would I eat lunch with you guys when I

could eat with real people?" she'd replied when Ellie had asked her at the end of history to join the group. "Besides, I'd lose my appetite."

Now Cole drew a quick sketch in his sketchbook of Rosie standing in the cafeteria line, giving her a dragon's long snout with flames coming through her nostrils.

Ethan sat at the other end of the table from Cole. After everyone had gotten settled into their seats, he banged his lacrosse stick on the floor like a scepter and said, "Let's bring this meeting to order."

Cole sketched Ethan wearing a jeweled crown and a robe with a fur collar.

"As we all know, Mrs. H is in trouble," Ethan began, "and if she's not careful, she's about to get in bigger trouble."

"Does someone have an extra straw?" Carson asked. "I forgot to grab one for my milk."

Ethan waited patiently as Elizabeth reached across the table and handed Carson a straw. "You've probably heard by now that Mrs. Herrera got in trouble last year for letting a student spend the day at the zoo so she could work on a research project," he continued. "Mrs. H sent a note around to the other sixth-grade team teachers telling them that this girl"—he paused to glance at the notebook in front of him—"Lucy Yee, would be gone for the day. Lucy's parents were aware of the situation; in fact, her mother was the one who drove her to the zoo."

Henry, who was sitting to Ethan's left, leaned in so everyone could see him. "But the bureaucracy demands that paperwork be done!"

"Yeah, it does," Ethan agreed. "Mrs. H was supposed to submit forms to the administration, signed by herself and Lucy Yee's parents, explaining why this absence was necessary and"—he looked at his notebook again—"beneficial to the student across the curriculum."

"At least ten days in advance," Henry added.

Ethan nodded. "That is correct. According to my mom, who's on the PTA and good friends with the school secretary, Mrs. H failed to do so and received a disciplinary notice in her file. Then it was discovered that she had previously allowed another student to spend the day at the history museum, also for a class project, and an . . . an . . ."—Ethan looked at his notes again—"an addendum was added to the notice."

"Aka, she's on thin ice," Henry clarified.

Cole drew Henry as a court jester. He put one of those funny hats on his head, the kind with three floppy, pointy things on top. Studying the sketch, Cole realized the hat was missing something and added little jingle bells to the end of each pointy thing. There. Much better.

"I'm really afraid she's going to get fired," Ariana said. "I mean, she's doing all these crazy things! Letting Sam Hawkins live in her classroom? He's homeless! We can't have a homeless kid living in our classroom, even a nice homeless kid!"

"Don't be an idiot," said Matt, who was sitting to Ethan's right. "First of all, Sam's not living in our classroom. People have seen him leaving school in the afternoon. Second, who says he's homeless?"

Cole drew Matt as an aggressive gorilla in a football uniform, with the words *Sometimes even I make a good point* coming out of his mouth and floating toward Ariana, who Cole had drawn as a Chihuahua with a flowery backpack.

Elizabeth, who was sitting next to Ariana, said in a quiet voice, "I saw him at the homeless shelter near the Hope Valley Shopping Center when Petra and I were dropping off clothes there this weekend. He wasn't doing work like the people who volunteer there. And I volunteer there with my mom a lot, so I think I would have seen him before if he was a volunteer. When I saw him, he was eating lunch and reading a book, and this sad lady was sitting next to him. I think it was his mom."

"Okay, homeless/not homeless. Either way, why's he spending so much time over here?" Carson asked. "He's supposed to be at another school. Dudes, he moved, remember?"

"Is he here right now?" Stefan asked. "Because most people have seen him before or after school. Only Ellie has seen him during school. So maybe he's just coming back to visit. Maybe the day Ellie saw him, his new school had a teacher workday."

Ben crumpled up his lunch bag and stood. "I'll go

look and see if he's in the classroom now. Let's agree that if he's here, we have a problem. If he's not, then Stefan's probably right—he just likes coming around before or after school to see Mrs. Herrera. Maybe they bonded before he moved."

"You can't go until recess," Cammi, who was sitting next to Carson, pointed out. "You're not allowed in the hallways."

"It's me, okay?" Ben said. "As long as I stay in the sixth-grade wing, who's going to stop me?"

"Fair enough, dude," Carson said, and Cole drew Carson and Cammi as two peas in a pod, except that that Carson was a pea and Cammi was a lima bean. *The same, but different,* he wrote underneath their picture.

"Have you ever noticed that guys like Ben get away with a lot of stuff?" Rogan asked as everyone watched Ben walk out the cafeteria doors without one teacher asking him for a pass or wanting to know where he was going. "It's like if you're a genius and you stay pretty quiet, teachers don't care what you do or where you go."

"It pays to have a brain," Bart said. "Just ask Bill Gates, am I right?"

"Shut it, dude," Matt said. "Am I right?"

"Why don't you shut it?" Garrison asked Matt. "Bart didn't say anything wrong."

Cole glanced around the table and then drew a sea of faces, eyes wide and mouths hanging open. One thing was for sure, he thought as he drew a picture of Superman. Only Garrison could get away with saying *that*.

He gave Superman Garrison's face.

"So what's the point of this meeting anyway?" Matt asked, a red flush edging above his collar. "Because it's getting boring."

Ethan banged his stick again. "Okay, good question. Here's another question: Who here wants to see Mrs. H get fired? Show of hands."

Nobody's hand went up. "Me either," Ethan said. "But if Sam's really hanging out in her classroom during the day, whether he's homeless or not, and she gets caught letting him hang out . . ." Ethan drew his finger across his neck. "That's it. She's out of here."

Aadita raised her hand. When Ethan pointed at her, she said, "If it is true she's hiding Sam in her classroom, what I would like to know is *why*? I mean, why is she taking this risk?"

"She's too soft," Garrison offered. "She lets people get to her too easily."

Becca, who was sitting next to Matt, harrumphed. "Don't let Mrs. Herrera fool you."

"Have you talked to her yet?" Matt asked Becca in a low voice, and when Becca shook her head, he said, "Then maybe you don't know what's going on with her. Remember what I told you?"

Becca nodded glumly. "I need to go talk to her."

Ben reappeared at the table. "He's in there," he said a little breathlessly. "And she is too—Mrs. Herrera. She's sitting at her desk and he's sitting in the back row, writing something in a notebook. I tried the door, but it's locked."

"So can anybody explain this situation?" Ethan asked the group. "And then tell us what to do?"

No one said anything for a minute. Elizabeth looked at Ariana, who shrugged, like *Don't look at me*. Cammi looked at Carson, and Carson looked at Ben. Garrison glanced at Felicity, who blushed and looked down at her lap. Ellie looked at Cole, who drew a picture of Sam and Mrs. Herrera hiding out in a World War II–style bunker. Ethan raised an eyebrow at Bart, who tapped Stefan on the shoulder. "Come on, Stef. You're good at this kind of thing. Explain why Mrs. Herrera would do this."

Stefan was quiet for a moment. "I don't know," he said finally. "I mean, unless Sam's really in our class again, he shouldn't be here. Mrs. Herrera knows that. But maybe his new school sucks. Or maybe it's like Elizabeth says, and he lives with his mom in a homeless shelter and is really unhappy. Maybe Mrs. Herrera is trying to figure out a plan, but she hasn't yet. But I'm with everybody else—I don't want her to get fired. So the next question is, what do we do?"

Nobody said anything for a long time, and then Cole looked up from his sketchbook. "We form a human shield," he said. He held up the picture he'd just drawn—an enormous shield held up by a big group of people. You couldn't see the people's faces, though, only their feet.

"Explain," said Ben, who was still standing next to Ethan.

But before Cole could explain, Ellie jumped in. "We all stand in front of him, so that no one can see him."

"Sort of," Cole said. "It's more of a blending-in thing. If we all go sit at our desks right now, who's going to notice Sam? He's just another kid. We could probably take him out on the playground and play soccer. He looks like at least two other kids I can think of— James Falter, who's in Mrs. Logan's homeroom, and this other guy—"

"George Chaggs," Garrison interrupted, nodding with excitement. "You know, that kid in Mr. Lee's class? He's the second-string quarterback on my travel team."

"So if some teacher sees him from a distance, she just thinks it's James or George," Ellie said. "You're a genius, Cole!"

Cole bowed to Ellie. "Thank you," he said. "It

was about time one of you guys figured that out."

"Okay, let's go," Garrison said, standing. "Let's go form a shield."

Ben pointed at the clock on the wall. "We need to wait two more minutes. We'll draw more attention if we try to leave early, especially as a group. The point is *not* to draw attention to ourselves or to Sam."

"I hear you," Garrison said. "Good point."

"But by all means, lead the way when it's time," Ben said, and Garrison nodded. It was like watching generals from two different armies join forces, Cole thought. He drew a picture of Ben and Garrison standing next to each other, each in military uniforms. Ben had a badge on his chest that read *Geek Army*. Garrison's said *Jock Brigade*.

"But we shouldn't all walk together, like Ben said," Felicity pointed out. "In fact, we should go in different directions and then circle back around. Try not to look suspicious."

Cole sketched Felicity dressed in a black trench coat with a black fedora pulled low on her forehead.

The recess bell rang. "Okay, everybody," Garrison

said. "Break into groups, but be back in the classroom in two minutes."

"Two minutes, everyone!" Henry repeated. "Two minutes! That's one-two-and-not-three minutes!"

And to Cole's amazement, nobody told him to shut up.

Chapter Twenty-Two

Felicity

Wednesday, October 18

As soon as the bell rang, Felicity, Rogan, and Cole exited the cafeteria, walked to the library, stopped, turned around, and headed for the classroom. When they got there, Mrs. Herrera was pacing at the front of the room, arms crossed, looking anxious. For the first time ever, she didn't seem like she was in charge of the class, which made Felicity feel nervous. Mrs. Herrera might be nice and she might be reasonable and understanding, but she was *always* in charge.

Garrison and Ben, who were both tall, were sitting at the desks in front of Sam, who was sitting in the middle of the back row. Ellie sat to Sam's left, Ethan to his right.

"You guys start filling in the desks around Sam," Garrison instructed as Felicity's group walked through the door. "Don't worry about whose seat you're sitting in."

"We're doing this back to front," Ben added. "Let's focus on blocking Sam from view."

Felicity sat down in the desk next to Ellie. "Has Mrs. Herrera said anything yet?" she whispered.

"She just asked us why we wanted to come in during recess," Ellie whispered back. "We told her we were having a class meeting and would explain after everyone got here."

More of the class filed in, Ethan followed by Stefan followed by Bart followed by Elizabeth followed by Adriana followed by Henry. Felicity felt a shiver of excitement as she watched people silently take their seats. Something was happening here. Something important. Until this week, she wouldn't have been here to be a part of it. She would have been on the playground with Madeline and Anna.

So maybe it was for the best that they were no longer friends.

Felicity had hated sixth grade from the minute she'd gotten her homeroom assignment. Everyone in Mrs. Herrera's class was either a total dweeb or a total jerk, and the idea of having to travel from class to class with Henry Lloyd? Unbearable. Putting up with Becca Hobbes's goody-goody routine for yet another year? Too irritating for words. Garrison was a snob, Matt was a bully, and Bart Weems was a geek and had zits. He'd had zits in fifth grade! Gross.

Worst of all, Madeline and Anna weren't there. No, worst of all, Madeline and Anna were together in Mr. Lee's homeroom. Felicity wasn't fooling herself: this was bad news. This was a big win for Anna. For the last two years, Anna and Felicity had been battling each other for the position of Madeline's best friend, and this was the break Anna had been waiting for. Between school and travel soccer, Anna now had total Madeline domination.

The problem was the inside joke, which was Anna's

specialty. They all might be eating lunch together in the cafeteria and talking about something they'd seen on TV the night before, when Anna would lean toward Madeline and say, "That reminds me—Josh McNabb candy!" Madeline would burst out laughing, and Anna would laugh like crazy, and Felicity would laugh like she was asking a question. *So why is that funny exactly?*

"Inside joke!" Anna would say in between giggles. "You wouldn't understand."

Felicity had hung in there for the first two months of sixth grade. She had one advantage over Anna, and that was car pool. She and Madeline and the horrible Henry Lloyd carpooled to and from school every day, a blissful Anna-free fifteen minutes each way. They had to put up with Henry, but Henry was better in small groups, so he wasn't always a pain, and in the mornings he was actually pretty quiet. Madeline was her old self in car pool, and she and Felicity talked about the things they always talked about—what they'd watched on TV the night before, what they'd seen on Pinterest or Instagram, who liked who, who was being a jerk, how much they hated PE.

And then one day, just like that, Madeline had dropped out of car pool and Felicity finally gave up.

Taking the bus in the morning, Madeline had texted the night before. My mom decided it's time. Anna takes the bus, so I think it's going to be okay.

Felicity and Madeline had sworn they'd never take the bus to middle school. They'd heard the rumors about what happened on the bus, and so had their moms. It wasn't just bra snapping or bad language, either. Madeline's mom had heard that two kids had been caught—well, she wouldn't give the details on what they'd been doing, but it hadn't been good.

Wow, Felicity had texted back. Just wow.

I'm excited! Jason Weatherford rides the bus too!

Okay, now it made sense. Madeline and Anna were both madly in love with Jason Weatherford, captain of the seventh-grade soccer team. As long as he was on the bus, Madeline would never carpool again.

The next morning when they picked up Henry, Felicity had expected him to make a big deal about Madeline not being there—not because he cared, but because Henry was always looking for an excuse to make a big deal over something. To her surprise, he was quiet when he got into the car and didn't say a word for the first ten minutes.

As they got close to school, Henry had leaned forward and tapped Felicity on the shoulder. "Could you do me a favor?" he asked. "A very not-hard-to-do favor?"

"What?" Felicity asked, wondering what Henry could possible want her help with.

He passed a notebook to her. "Give this to Ellie. I accidentally picked it up yesterday, but if I give it back to her, she'll think I stole it on purpose."

"It's just a notebook," Felicity pointed out. "Why would she think you would bother stealing a notebook?"

"People are very suspicious of me no matter what I do or how much I proclaim my innocence," Henry replied.

Felicity had shoved the notebook in her backpack and promptly forgotten all about it. It wasn't until that night when she was getting out her math book that she remembered. She didn't know what made her open

Ellie's notebook and look inside, but once she did, she couldn't stop reading.

On the first page, all it said was *The Class*. On the second page, the notes began:

> *It's not just that Stefan is smart, it's that he seems interested in everything. Unlike Ben, who's also really smart but acts like he'd rather be somewhere else.*

> *I don't think Petra and Rosie actually like each other. They're like two powerful countries, and the only reason they're friends is because they're more powerful together.*

> *People say Garrison is stuck-up, and I can totally see that. But the other day I was talking to my mom, and when I said, "There's this boy in our class who's a really good football player and he's cute and he acts stuck-up," she said,*

"Maybe he's shy." And now when I look at Garrison, he really does seem shy.

Today in math, I heard Ariana tell Elizabeth that Aadita's mom is some kind of genius scientist. I wonder if Aadita is a genius too. Maybe that's why she never talks—she's got too many genius thoughts going on in her mind.

In a way, I don't think Carson makes a very good popular person. He's not mean or mysterious. He's really cute, and I guess he uses his looks to get stuff (he came over to me at lunch the other day and asked if he could have my cupcake, which is probably the first time he's said anything to me all year!), but he acts pretty nice in general. I think if you're a boy, being cute and a good athlete is enough to make you popular.

If you're a girl, you have to be able to make other people scared of you.

Sometimes I wonder if boys are better at being friends than girls. Rogan and Ethan and Cole don't seem like they'd ever fight or give each other the silent treatment.

I wonder if Henry Lloyd is lonely.

Who is Felicity Wallack? She hardly talks in class, although she's got the answer whenever a teacher calls on her. But when I see her in the cafeteria with Madeline and Anna, she talks a lot. Sometimes she looks sort of desperate, though. Like if she stopped talking, she'd drown.

When she read that, Felicity had to put the note-book down. Was that really how she looked around Madeline and Anna? Desperate? She had to admit it: that was how she felt. Like if she stopped talking, she'd disappear into thin air and Madeline and Anna wouldn't even notice.

After dinner, Felicity picked up the notebook again and read through the whole thing. She was hoping Ellie would say something about more about her, but her name didn't come up again. Ellie spent a lot of time wondering about Becca and about Petra Wilde (who Ellie thought had cut her hair so she could stop being Petra Wilde, which Felicity had to admit made sense— Petra always seemed dissatisfied to her, like she was the girl who had everything, but she didn't want everything, she wanted something else), and she was mildly fascinated by Bart Weems, of all people (Ellie wondered why no one ever seemed to notice that Bart actually had a very pleasant personality and a good sense of humor).

Ellie's notes struck Felicity as being true without being mean. It was true that Ariana's niceness seemed like a costume she put on every morning (Felicity thought this was a perfect way to put it), and it was true that if Stefan's outside matched his insides, he'd be the best-looking boy in their class, but life was totally unfair that way and so he looked like someone you'd only want to be friends with.

Felicity wished she and Ellie were friends. Because here it was, nearly two months into the sixth grade, and Felicity Wallack could use a friend.

It took her almost a week to return the notebook. She hadn't planned on asking Ellie to eat lunch with her when she did, but as soon as she did, she felt a sense of relief washing over her. If they ate lunch together, Ellie would have something to write about her, and then Felicity wouldn't be invisible anymore.

By the time everyone had gotten back to the classroom and taken a seat, it really was like there was a shield around Sam Hawkins. Felicity imagined Mrs. Whalen poking her head in the door to ask why the class was spending recess inside. She'd never notice Sam in a million years. For now at least, Sam was safe, and so was Mrs. Herrera.

Now people were starting to look around at each other, like they were asking, *What next?* Finally Ellie cleared her throat and raised her hand. "Mrs. Herrera?"

"Yes, Ellie?" said Mrs. Herrera, still pacing.

"We'd like to ask some questions, if that's okay," Ellie said.

Mrs. Herrera finally stopped moving. She nodded at Ellie.

"Well, is it okay if we ask what Sam's doing here? Because he moved, right?"

It took Mrs. Herrera a moment to say anything. Finally she said, "Do you want to answer that, Sam?"

Everyone turned around to look at Sam, who was looking down at his hands. He shook his head.

"Is it okay if I answer it?"

Sam nodded without looking up.

Mrs. Herrera walked over to her desk and leaned against it. "Yes, Sam did move, but only a mile away— into another school district, but not another town. He's been coming back to visit me while he's making the transition to his new school."

Ellie raised her hand. "I saw him here during lunch period last week. Is Sam hiding out here?"

"No, he is not hiding out here," Mrs. Herrera said. She seemed to be relaxing a little. "This is only the second time he's come to the classroom."

"Isn't that against the rules?" Becca asked.

(*Typical Becca question,* Felicity thought.)

"Yes, Sam and I have discussed that," Mrs. Herrera said. "It's one thing for him to come see me before or after school. It's another thing for him to be in this classroom when he should be elsewhere. It won't happen again."

Garrison raised his hand. "Is it true that Sam's homeless?"

Mrs. Herrera paused and took a deep breath. Everyone turned again to look at Sam. Sam looked back at everyone, and Felicity noticed his ears had turned so red they were almost purple. He nodded.

"You might be surprised to know how easy it is to fall through the cracks," Mrs. Herrera said. "Sam's mom lost her job in June and couldn't pay rent. She found a new job in September, but it can take a while to earn enough to pay a first and last month's deposit on an apartment. For now, she and Sam have to live in a shelter."

"Why doesn't Sam hang out at his own school?" Bart asked. "I mean, I don't mind him being here, but why not go where you're supposed to go?"

"It sucks," Sam said, and everyone turned to stare at him. "Especially LA. All we do is grammar. You have no idea how lucky you are to be in this class."

Mrs. Herrera took a few steps so she was standing in front of the class, and Felicity wondered if she was trying to get everyone's attention off Sam. "Sam comes here sometimes in the afternoon and writes and does homework while I do my prep for the next day."

"I saw him in the bathroom on Friday morning," Henry said. "Which, strictly speaking, isn't Friday afternoon."

"I don't like the bathroom at the shelter," Sam said. "And there's a lady in the cafeteria here who gives me breakfast."

"That's a long way to come for breakfast, bro," Matt pointed out.

"Sometimes she brings cinnamon rolls from home."

Felicity turned to look at Sam. "I saw you this morning behind the building. Are you coming here and staying all day?"

"Not in this classroom, no," Sam answered. "But sometimes I hang around. There's eight hundred students at this school. No one really notices."

Felicity shook her head. It was bad enough going unnoticed by your two so-called best friends. Imagine going unnoticed by eight hundred people. Whoa.

"We can't stop you from coming here," Ben said, turning around so he was facing Sam directly. "But you could get Mrs. Herrera in a lot of trouble."

"Maybe you should stop hanging out in the classroom during lunch," Garrison added. "Maybe you could hang out with us on the playground instead?"

"Just put up the hood of your hoodie," Stefan said. "No one will ever realize who you are."

"If they even remember in the first place," Sam said, scowling.

"I remember you," said Ariana in a quiet voice. "I thought it was sad when you left."

Felicity leaned back in her seat. So Ariana had feelings that weren't a hundred percent chirpy and positive. So maybe she was human after all. Interesting.

Ethan raised his hand. "Mrs. Herrera, are you going to get in trouble for not telling someone Sam is here?"

"I'm working on a plan to help Sam," Mrs. Herrera said, but her expression was a little less than confident. "But yes, I could get in a lot of trouble."

Ethan turned to Sam. "Come on, dude, let's go outside."

Garrison and Ben stood and walked to the door. "Okay, guys," Garrison said. "It's time."

Felicity watched as everyone crowded around the door. Ellie led Sam up the aisle and gently pushed him into the middle of the group. "Hoodie up, Sam," she instructed, and Sam pulled his hood up over his head. Felicity stood up then and walked around the island of desks to the front of the classroom. She passed Mrs. Herrera, whose face was a mix of wonder and worry and—well, maybe pride, Felicity thought. It looked complicated, whatever she was feeling.

"This is a good class," Felicity said as she followed the group out of the room, turning to smile at Mrs. Herrera before she walked out the door.

"It's a very good class," Mrs. Herrera agreed, sounding like she'd never doubted it for a minute. "I'm glad you're back."

Chapter Twenty-Three

Elizabeth

Monday, October 23

"I think what you should do is some stream-of-consciousness writing," Mrs. Herrera told Elizabeth when she'd gone in for help with her book report during recess on Monday. "Take a seat at the Editor's Roundtable and try to remember some of the thoughts you had while you were reading the book. Look over your reading journal. Don't worry about getting it right or about analyzing. Just get your feelings down on paper. We'll take it from there."

Elizabeth took her LA notebook and her reading journal to the back of the classroom. She hated writing papers about books she loved, because she hated having to pick them apart and write stuff like, *There are three important themes in this book,* or *Some of the symbols the author uses in this book include* . . . Books weren't about themes and symbols! Books were about people. On Friday, Garrison had done a book report on *Hatchet,* and he'd talked about the main character, Brian, like he was an actual person, a close, personal friend. Elizabeth totally got that.

(Was Garrison the one who'd stolen *Hatchet* from Mrs. Herrera's special collection? Mrs. Herrera wasn't saying who brought her special signed copy back, but Elizabeth had her suspicions.)

The sounds of basketballs hitting backboards and feet pounding across the pavement filtered in through an open window behind Mrs. Herrera's desk. Elizabeth knew if she got up and looked out, she'd see almost everyone in their class playing soccer on the far edge of the sports field. Would Sam be there? Every morning now there was an unofficial Sam report—had anybody seen him yet? If so, had they made sure he had something to eat, maybe a book to read?—but no one had seen him so far today. That didn't mean he wouldn't show up. Last week he didn't come around on Thursday, but he was there on Friday at lunch, waiting outside at the far end of the soccer field, hood pulled up so no one would recognize him.

Elizabeth wondered how much longer Sam would show up. He had to start going to his new school sooner or later, didn't he? He'd told Ethan on Friday that a lot of kids who stayed at the shelter didn't go to school on a regular basis. "He says it's hard to do your homework at the shelter," Ethan reported to the class after lunch. "And some kids don't like leaving their moms all alone. In Sam's case, he'd just rather be here."

But sooner or later, Elizabeth thought now, he'd have to be *there*—at his other school, right?

She opened her reading journal to an entry about whether she would have been Auggie's friend if she'd been a character in *Wonder*. She'd written that she hoped she would be, but was afraid she might have been too worried about what other people thought. That made her feel ashamed, because she wanted to be a nice person, not someone who cared about people's looks.

What's more important, how a person looks or how they act? she wrote, and then she erased it. Blah. Of course the answer was how a person acts, everybody knew that. Elizabeth didn't want to write something boring. She wanted to write about how the book made her feel, but she didn't know how to put her feelings into sentences and paragraphs. Sometimes at night she liked to sit at the piano and make up little tunes that matched her mood, and Elizabeth wished she could do that for this paper instead of having to use words. She started tapping out pretend notes on the table, *da da daa, de de—*

"We need to talk!"

Becca exploded into the room, heading straight for Mrs. Herrera's desk, and there was something about the way she moved—like an animal that had been caged up for a long time or a ball thrown hard from one side of the room to the other—that made Elizabeth want to hide under the table. It definitely didn't seem like the right time to say hi, so she bent her head lower over her notebook and tried to be invisible.

"Matt told me I should ask you something, and

I guess I'm going to," Becca said, panting a little as though she'd been running. "When school first started, like for the first month, I brought you stuff. I was trying to be nice—" Becca stopped, mumbled to herself, then continued. "I was trying to make you like me. But you never ate any of the snacks I gave you. You didn't eat one single Oreo. It's like you didn't even care. And it really hurt my feelings."

Elizabeth lifted her head slightly so she could see Becca. Becca's eyes were red; she looked like she might start crying at any second.

"Becca," Mrs. Herrera said softly. She looked like she might cry too. "I'm so sorry. I should have said something to you earlier, but when you stopped bringing me gifts, well, I guess I thought I didn't need to."

Becca stared at the ground. "What were you going to say to me? I mean, if I'd kept bringing you stuff?"

Mrs. Herrera seemed to think about this, as though she wanted to use the exact right words. "I would have told you that I appreciated the gifts you gave me," she said after a moment. "And maybe I would have told you that there are two reasons I didn't eat the snacks. One,

I'm very careful about not having favorites. You are the sort of student I appreciate very much. You work hard, you help out in the classroom, and you do your best. But to make you my favorite would be unfair to the other students. So I kept the things you gave me to remind myself that no matter how much I appreciated you, I couldn't allow myself to like you more than my other students."

"Really?" Becca asked with a sniff. "But if you did have a favorite, it would be me?"

Mrs. Herrera stood up and walked around her desk so that she was standing by Becca's side. "I think you should stop trying so hard to be your teachers' favorite. I think you should believe your teachers will like you for just being Becca Hobbes."

Becca nodded. "Maybe," she said. "That's sort of what Matt said."

Mrs. Herrera smiled. "I've noticed that you and Matt have become friends. Interestingly, he seems to have been a good influence on you. I hope you'll be a good influence on him."

"I'm trying," Becca said. She sighed and shook her

head. "It's not easy. So what's the second reason?"

"The second reason I didn't eat the snacks you gave me—even though I love Oreos very much—is that my doctor told me that I'm prediabetic and that I needed to stop eating sugar and junk food."

"I didn't know!" Becca gasped. "I never would have given you those things if I'd known!"

"It's perfectly okay," Mrs. Herrera said. "And I'm perfectly okay. Sadly, my days of eating Oreos are behind me. I would appreciate you not telling the rest of the class about my condition. It's private information that I'm sharing with you because I know I can trust you."

Elizabeth wondered if she should slip under the table and try to sneak out of the room. She hadn't been trying to eavesdrop, well, not really. Okay, sort of. But now she wished she'd left when Becca came in.

"You, too, Elizabeth," Mrs. Herrera called over. "I'm going to trust you to keep this private."

"You can trust Elizabeth," Becca said authoritatively. "She won't tell."

That was so Becca Hobbes—always the expert! True,

Elizabeth was pretty sure she could be trusted, though she still decided to go straight home after school instead of to Ariana's, just in case the temptation to tell Mrs. Herrera's secret became too much.

"There's one other thing I want to ask you about," Becca said to Mrs. Herrera, and Mrs. Herrera nodded for her to go ahead. "Why haven't you told anyone that Sam is here and not at his new school? Isn't that wrong? I mean, you're a teacher. You're a grown-up."

Mrs. Herrera didn't say anything for a minute. Elizabeth wondered if this was another conversation she shouldn't overhear, but she was dying to know the answer. No one in the class could figure it out. Mrs. Herrera was such a stickler for rules, but wasn't she breaking a huge one by not telling someone that Sam was here and not where he was supposed to be?

Mrs. Herrera walked back to her desk and sat down. "I'll be honest with you, Becca, since you've been honest with me. This is a situation where I'm not sure what the right thing to do is. If I want to stick to the letter of the law, then I should report to the front office that Sam is spending time on school grounds when he should be at his new school. I know that I'm breaking the rules by not telling anyone about Sam."

"Which means you're wrong."

Mrs. Herrera nodded. "Yes, I believe so. But the first day Sam went to his new school, someone took his notebook—the one he writes his stories in—and threw it in the toilet. He was also put in remedial classes, even though he's a very bright student. Apparently they put all the shelter kids in remedial classes. So I'm working through back channels to reenroll him here, even though he's no longer in this school district."

A thought occurred to Elizabeth, but she wasn't sure if she was part of this conversation. Still, it seemed important. "Mrs. Herrera? What would happen if you *did* report that Sam was here?"

"That's the funny thing," Mrs. Herrera replied with a sad smile. "I think what would happen is—nothing. Nothing except that the security team would be told to keep an eye out for him."

"So you have to wonder, why bother to report it at all?" Becca said. "It doesn't change anything."

"That's what I've been grappling with," Mrs. Herrera

said. "I really don't know if I'm doing the right thing or not."

Becca nodded. "Sometimes rules aren't very helpful."

Elizabeth nearly fell out of her seat. Those were the last words she ever thought she'd hear coming out of Becca Hobbes's mouth. She couldn't wait to tell Ariana . . . except that Ariana might roll her eyes and say something—well, something that sounded nice on its surface but was really meanness disguised as niceness. It would sort of ruin this moment when Elizabeth thought about it again. Which she planned on doing, because it was one of the more interesting moments she'd had lately.

"Okay then," Becca said, and Elizabeth thought she sounded like she'd run out of steam. "I guess I'm going to go play soccer. But, Mrs. Herrera?"

"Yes, Becca?"

"My next-door neighbor, Mrs. Quentin, is pretty old and she's looking for a live-in companion. Do you think Sam's too young to do that? Because if he lived with Mrs. Quentin, he'd be back in our school district."

Mrs. Herrera started to laugh. "Oh, Becca! Yes, Sam's

too young—" Then she stopped short and her eyes went wide. "But his mother's not. Could you e-mail me Mrs. Quentin's contact information? Maybe she and Sam's mom could talk."

Later Elizabeth would swear that even though it was a cloudy day, a beam of sunlight had come through the window and lit up Becca's face. "I'll do it as soon as I get home! And Mrs. Herrera, when I do? Would you e-mail my mom and tell her you're happy I'm in your class this year? Because . . . well, that's what my teachers usually do." Now Becca stopped short, bit her lower lip. "You don't have to say I'm your favorite or anything. You just have to say I've been good."

Mrs. Herrera looked like she might cry again. "Becca, I'll send that e-mail right now," she said, turning to her computer. "And I'll also tell her how much I love your new haircut."

Becca grinned. "I look pretty awesome, don't I?"

"You got something in the mail," her grandmother said when Elizabeth walked into the kitchen that afternoon. "Strike that. Someone left you something in the mailbox. It wasn't actually mailed. No stamps on it, anyway."

"You're confusing me, Bela," Elizabeth said. "I've got mail that isn't mail?"

"Isn't that what I just said? It's on the counter next to the toaster. What do you want for snack? Peanut butter on apple slices?"

"Maybe later," Elizabeth said. "My teacher gave me some Oreos she had in her desk."

"Not stale Oreos, I hope."

Elizabeth laughed. "A little stale, but still good."

The envelope on the counter was large and padded. Someone had printed her name and address on it, but there was no return address. It was all very mysterious.

"So, open it!" Bela said, sitting down at the kitchen table with a cup of coffee. "Aren't you dying to see what's inside?"

"It's probably nothing," Elizabeth said, wishing her grandmother wasn't so nosy. She'd rather take the envelope upstairs and think about what it might be for a little while. It probably *was* nothing, but who knew? Maybe it was something. Maybe it was a gift from a secret admirer, or, or—a ransom note! Not that she was aware of anything (or anyone) missing, but maybe somebody had stolen her bike out the garage or taken one of the garden gnomes without anyone noticing.

"Open and see!" her grandmother urged. "It's been a boring day around here. I could use some excitement."

Elizabeth carried the envelope over to the table and sat down. Usually she was glad Bela had moved in with them over the summer—it meant she didn't have to go to extended-day study hall after school, for one thing—but on days like today, she wished she could have a little privacy. Bela wasn't very big on privacy.

She carefully peeled back the flap and gently shook the envelope. A folded piece of notebook paper taped to a picture frame slid out. She unstuck the paper and unfolded it.

"Read it!" her grandmother ordered. "I want to know what it says."

Elizabeth held up her hand. "I'm going to read it to myself. Maybe it's personal."

Her grandmother sighed. "If you're going to be that way, I'm going upstairs. It's time for *Love It or List It.*"

Elizabeth waited until she heard Bela's footsteps on the stairs to read the note. She didn't recognize the handwriting, though clearly it belonged to a girl. Should she peek at the bottom? No, she wanted to be surprised.

Dear Elizabeth, the note began.

Enclosed please find the photograph of Mrs. Abbott, our esteemed teacher's favorite teacher. In case you're wondering, I didn't steal it; I just received it from Lila's backpack. There's a difference. Two of my former colleagues did, though who knows why. Probably because they're idiots.

I have two favors to ask of you. Why you? Because you are probably one of two friends I currently have. Did you know that we were friends? All it took was five boxes full of used clothes and a trip to the homeless shelter. We didn't even talk that much, but I was watching you the whole time, how you joked around with the little kids who wanted to help us put the clothes in the right piles and spoke Spanish to some old lady who got confused and thought you were her daughter.

I didn't know you could speak Spanish or even that you knew how to make jokes. I wish I'd known those things. Do you ever wish we could know the insides of other people, that we could know everything that goes on in their heads? Or even what they eat when they go home. What does Bart eat for dinner? Does his mom like to cook? Maybe his dad does all the cooking for their family. I don't know, do you?

Over the last few days I've been thinking about the people in our class, and I've made some decisions. For instance, I've decided that you try to be nice, but you're not really nice. Niceness is fake. It's like frosting on a cake. The cake might taste great or it might taste horrible. The frosting makes you think it's great on the inside, but who knows for sure?

I don't think you're a fake person. I don't think you're a nice person. I think you're a good person, which is better than nice.

Do you know who else I think is good? Becca Hobbes. Her problem is that she wants to advertise her goodness all the time. She's good, but she's a show-off. What I like about you is that you don't advertise.

I also think you're kind, which is different from good. Becca isn't kind. Neither is Ariana. She's nice, but not kind.

Because you're good and you're kind, I'm asking you two favors. One is, would you please put this photograph in the lost and found? If you put it in an envelope marked "Mrs. Herrera," it will get returned to her sooner or later.

Two, would you please ask Stefan to the Fall Ball? We were supposed to go together, but I'm at a different school now, so I can't. I think you and Stefan have a lot in common. If you don't believe me, watch how he acts with Henry. He's more than nice. He's not showing off. He's good.

Believe it or not, I'd like to be good. I know I'm mean, but being mean is like being nice. It's just a different kind of frosting. Being good, that's the cake.

You're a good cake. I hope you have a good life.

If you ever find out what Bart eats for dinner, let me know.

Sincerely,
Petra Wilde

Elizabeth's heart was racing when she finished the note. Petra Wilde had thought about her? Had spent time thinking about Elizabeth Hernandez? It was actually sort of a scary realization. As a general rule of thumb, you didn't want someone like Petra to know you even existed. It was like a hawk realizing a sparrow existed. Bye-bye, sparrow. Better luck next time.

But you're still here, Elizabeth told herself, looking around the kitchen. *Safe in your house. And for some reason Petra Wilde thinks you're good.*

Elizabeth didn't feel like a good person, exactly. She knew she'd done some bad things. She'd taken money from her mom's purse so she could buy candy at the school store, and sometimes she copied Ariana's math homework. She tried to stay away from people like Henry Lloyd, who she thought was a little bit crazy. Elizabeth wasn't sure that Petra knew her well enough to say whether she was good or bad.

It was interesting, though, what Petra said about the difference between good and nice. And that idea that you could be mean and good? Elizabeth didn't know what she thought about that, but she wanted to think about it some more.

She did think Stefan Morrisey was kind. He was also short and overweight, and Elizabeth didn't know if she wanted to go to the dance with him.

If she were good, she'd want to.

If she were good, she'd text Stefan right now and ask him.

Elizabeth stood up and walked over to the fridge. She was afraid it was true: if someone who looked really strange or deformed came to her school, she probably wouldn't be friends with them. Petra was wrong. Elizabeth was nice, but she wasn't good.

But you could try to be good, she thought as she grabbed a piece of string cheese from the refrigerator.

At least you could try to be better.

She sat back down at the kitchen table and pulled out her LA notebook. *Nice versus Good,* she wrote at the top of the page. *A Few of My Thoughts on the Book* Wonder.

And then she put down her pen and picked up her phone.

Chapter Twenty-Four

Ellie

Saturday, October 28

Ellie felt itchy. Usually when she felt itchy it meant she wanted to write something but didn't have her pen and notebook. Right now she felt itchy because she was wearing a dress. And standing in the school gym on a Saturday night without a notebook. Or a pen. Or any idea how to dance.

"Have you ever been to a dance before?" Felicity was standing next to Ellie, also in a dress, also looking like she felt a little itchy. "Because I haven't, and I'm not sure what to do. We can't just stand here all night, can we?"

"We could," Ellie said. "But what's the point of spending five dollars on a ticket if we're just going to stand here?"

"Should we start dancing?" Felicity asked.

"Maybe we should mingle first." Ellie pointed to the refreshments table, where Ethan, Rogan, and Cole seemed to be having a contest for who could stuff the most pizza in their mouths. "How about we start with those guys?"

"Ethan looks different without his lacrosse stick," Felicity observed as they crossed the gym. "It's like Harry Potter without his glasses."

"And Cole looks kind of strange not carrying a sketchbook around," Ellie said. "I'd like to see how he'd draw everybody here."

"At least the people we know," Felicity agreed. "Which is not that many. Why aren't there more sixth graders?"

Ellie shrugged. Good question. Well, most of Mrs. Herrera's class was here, but that was how it had been with their class lately. They'd gotten in the habit of showing up in the same places, at the playground first thing in the morning, at the same cluster of tables at lunch, at the soccer field during recess. Rosie still kept away, and Lila did too, mostly. But Ellie had seen Lila on the playground yesterday morning, standing at the edge of the popular girls, looking over at where the rest of the class was hanging out. Ellie had almost waved her over, and for the rest of the day she was sort of sorry she hadn't.

Looking around now, she saw Ariana, Elizabeth, and Stefan dancing together in a group at the edge of the dance floor. Bart and Ben stood nearby, checking out something on Ben's phone. Ellie wondered if it was true that Elizabeth had asked Stefan to the dance. Henry had been going around saying that Petra and Stefan had planned to go to the dance together before Petra had changed schools, but that was pretty hard to believe.

Even harder to believe was that Carson was supposed to come to the dance with Lila. The rumor was that she'd asked him. But what about Cammi? Ellie guessed that they were just friends after all. The news had broken on Thursday, and Cammi hadn't come to school yesterday, but now she was serving punch over at the refreshments table. Becca stood next to her, passing out the cups.

"Yo, Ellie!" Ethan called when he saw her, although it came out more like "O-ee-ee," because his mouth was stuffed with pizza. After he swallowed, he said, "Nice dress."

"Thanks," Ellie said. "It's the only one I've got."

"I told Cole I'd give him five dollars if he wore a skirt," Rogan said. "But he was too chicken."

"It's true, I do own a skirt," Cole said, wiping some tomato sauce from the corner of his mouth. "Well, strictly speaking, it's a kilt. My mom's big on our Scottish heritage."

"He rocks that skirt," Ethan said.

"Kilt," Cole corrected him.

"Moving on," Felicity said. She turned to Ellie. "Let's go see who else is here."

"We're coming with you," Rogan said. "If I eat any more pizza, I'm going to be sick."

"Should we head toward the basketball hoop?" Ellie asked, pointing to the other end of the gym. "Is that what you call that?"

"I think you call it a hoop if it's nailed to your garage," Ethan said. "In a gym, you call it a goal."

"I think it's the same thing either way," Cole said.

"You say kilt, I say skirt," Rogan said.

"You say skirt, I say hoop," said Henry, popping up from behind Felicity. "You say hoop, I say how high."

"Oh good, Henry's here," Ethan said dryly. "Dude, why aren't you dancing?"

"I'm waiting to fill my dance card," Henry said.

"That could take a while," Cole said.

"Ellie will dance with me, won't you?" Henry turned to Ellie and held out his hand. "They're playing our song."

Ellie felt her face go hot. She'd never danced with a boy before. She'd never danced period. Not in a room filled with other people, anyway. But she didn't want to hurt Henry's feelings, so she took a deep breath and said, "Sure. Okay."

Following Henry out onto the dance floor, Ellie could feel a million eyes staring at her. But when she actually looked around, no seemed to be paying her any attention at all. Even Felicity was too busy laughing at something Ethan had just said to make meaningful eye contact. *Okay,* Ellie thought, *I can do this. Just relax and move to the music, right?*

"I feel honor bound to tell you that if Aadita were here, I'd be dancing with her right now," Henry said. "Even though I think you're a nice person."

"She's not allowed to go to dances," Ellie informed him. "That's what she told me and Felicity. Her mom says sixth grade is too young."

"Or too old," Henry said. "Preschoolers make the best dancers. But that's sad about Aadita. I didn't know about her mom."

Henry didn't look sad, Ellie thought. He looked like Ellie had just given him some wonderful news. He also looked almost—relaxed? She had to admit he was a good dancer. Maybe it helped that dancing gave Henry's excess energy somewhere to go. Instead of dancing in one spot, she and Henry moved through the crowd, occasionally pausing so Henry could twirl Ellie around. After a few minutes, they'd circled around to the basketball goal, where Rogan, Cole, Cammi, and Ben were watching Ariana, Elizabeth, Becca, Stefan, Ethan, and Felicity dance.

"Are they having a hoedown without us?" Henry asked, twirling Ellie in the group's direction. "And why do you think a hoedown is called a hoedown? Is it because farmers had to put their hoes down to dance?"

When they reached the other dancers, Henry bowed. "Mind if we join you?"

The circle of dancers opened to let them in. Ellie felt more self-conscious dancing with the group—with Henry, dancing had felt like goofing around. With the rest of the group, dancing felt more personal, like people were letting you see a side of them they didn't usually let show.

Ellie shuffled back and forth, still looking around the gym. What was everyone thinking? Feeling? What could you really know about a person just by observing them at a middle-school dance? Was everyone nervous on the inside, even the people walking around looking superconfident? What was it really like to be Henry or Felicity or Stefan? What would Becca do when she got home? Drink hot cocoa with her mom and gossip with her about what everyone said and wore?

"Sam's here!" Elizabeth cried, pointing toward the

gym entrance, and then she started waving. "Sam! Sam! Over here!"

"He's wearing a tie!" Ariana said, sounding delighted. "That's so formal!"

Sam was leaning against a wall, his hands shoved into the pockets of his khaki pants. Finally he noticed Elizabeth waving at him. He waved back, but didn't move.

"They must have let him back in our school," Henry said. "They must have given him the key to the city!"

"He and his mom moved in with my neighbor yesterday," Becca informed them. "I helped carry some of their boxes, and I also baked them some cookies."

Ethan stopped dancing, a huge grin spreading across his face. "That means Sam's back in our school district and Mrs. Herrera is safe. No more thin ice."

That *was* good news, Ellie thought, and then wondered why such good news made her feel a little sad. Maybe it was because now the class wouldn't have to form a human shield around Sam anymore, to protect him and their teacher. Now Garrison could go back to the jock table and Ethan, Rogan, and Cole could sit over near the eighth-grade football team, and Ariana and Elizabeth could sit at their usual table by the window, and Ben, Stefan, and Bart could go back to the computer lab at recess, and Becca could head to the classroom to tidy up the book nook. Maybe Felicity would get bored with their class now that there wasn't some big drama going on and would start hanging out with Madeline and Anna again.

Ellie guessed if that happened, she'd go back to spending lunchtime at the library. The fact was she needed to get started on a new story, because it looked like this one had ended. The special things had been returned to the special collection, the mystery of Sam had been solved, he and his mom had a place to live, and Mrs. Herrera wouldn't get fired. As an added bonus, some people who hadn't been friends two weeks ago were friends now, or at least friendly.

So a happy ending, Ellie thought. But she wasn't happy. She didn't want to go back to the library, at least not at lunchtime. She didn't want Felicity to go back to Mr. Lee's class, or for Rogan, Ethan, and Cole to return to their table all the way on the other side of the cafeteria near the eighth-grade football players. She wanted the class to stay the class, the way it was right now.

"Come on," Elizabeth said. "Maybe if we all go over, he'll come and hang out with us."

Walking across the gym, Ellie thought that this could be the last scene of her book, everybody crossing the gym together, music thumping, laughter all around them, Sam waiting on the other side of the room, looking happy to be back.

Or it could be the first scene of her next book. Had she thought of that? Maybe nothing was ending.

Maybe her story was just beginning.

MRS. HERRERA'S SIXTH-GRADE CLASS *Front row (l-r)*: Mrs. Herrera, Ben, Lila; *second row (l-r)*: Rosie, Becca, Cole, Aadita, Stefan, Ariana; *third row (l-r)*: Rogan, Ellie, Cammi, Carson, Felicity, Henry; *back row (l-r)*: Matt, Sam, Petra, Bart, Elizabeth, Ethan, Garrison

MRS. HERRERA'S SIXTH-GRADE CLASS *Front row (l-r)*: Mrs. Herrera, Ben, Lila; *second row (l-r)*: Rosie, Becca, Cole, Aadita, Stefan, Ariana; *third row (l-r)*: Rogan, Ellie, Cammi, Carson, Felicity, Henry; *back row (l-r)*: Matt, Sam, Petra, Bart, Elizabeth, Ethan, Garrison

Acknowledgments

The author would like to thank the following people for their assistance, their brilliance, their wit, their fortitude, and their ongoing support in spite of their better judgment:

Caitlyn Dlouhy; Michelle Rosen; Alex Borbolla; Sonia Chaghatzbanian; Justin Chanda; Jeannie Ng; Irene Metaxatos; Kristin Esser; Elizabeth Blake-Linn; Amy Marie Stadelmann; and all of the Dowells, including Travis, the ever-faithful and affectionate pup.

Turn the page for a sneak peek at
Chicken Boy.

You might have heard about the time my granny got arrested on the first day of school. Maybe you were one of them pie-eyed kids she almost ran down with her 1984 sky blue Toyota truck, me riding shotgun. When Granny pulled up on the sidewalk like it was our own personal parking spot, everybody was yelling for them kids to get out of the way, but nobody could hear a thing over the blast of Granny's radio and her singing at the top of her lungs.

I sat in the police car while an officer made Granny walk a straight line with her finger on her nose, like maybe she'd been driving drunk, which she hadn't been. I wanted like anything to switch on the flashing lights, but the cop in the driver's seat seemed to guess what I had on my mind. "What's your name, son?" he asked, letting me know he was paying attention.

I looked at my reflection in his mirrored sunglasses. "Tobin McCauley."

The cop grinned and jerked his thumb toward Granny. "Is she a McCauley, too? Because that would explain everything right off the bat."

"She's the mother-in-law to a McCauley," I told him, my fingers still itching to hit that flashing-lights button.

"Close enough," is what the cop replied. I guess he meant anyone in spitting distance of being related to one of my brothers—or my sister, for that matter—had a good chance of having a criminal heart. Not that they ever got busted for anything too bad, mostly petty stuff like shoplifting and being a public nuisance. And Shane and Summer were so old now that they hardly ever did anything worse than jaywalk. It'd been years since Summer had lifted a lipstick from Eckerd drugstore, or Shane had gone hot-rodding the wrong way down Six Forks Road.

The cop eyed me suspiciously, remembering that I was a McCauley, too. "You get in much trouble?"

I tried to look tough. I'd stolen a few paper clips in my time, a pencil or two, been made to stay after school for cheating on a test. Most of the stuff I did, I did it because teachers seemed to expect it from me. If I didn't commit at least a few minor crimes, then they'd go on about how good I was, what a nice change from the other McCauleys they'd taught in years past. I hated school bad enough without the teachers making a fuss over me.

"Yeah, I get in trouble," I told the cop, puffing out my chest. "They had to put a special guard on me last year."

The cop gave me the quick once-over. "Bet there's not a prison built that could hold you, son," he said, then started choking on his own laughter, his face glowing red as a bowl of tomato soup.

Outside, Granny was making her case to the other officer. "I'm all this boy's got, 'cause his daddy's good for nothing," I heard her say.

"His mama passed on when he was seven. Somebody's got to take care of him."

"Yes, ma'am," the police officer agreed politely. "But that doesn't mean you don't have to follow proper parking procedures."

Granny shoved a piece of Juicy Fruit in her mouth. "You like that Alan Jackson? KISS Country Radio don't play nothing but that Alan Jackson, it seems like. I think he's right good-looking, but you can't see him on the radio, now can you?"

"That's right, ma'am," the officer said. He turned toward the squad car and rolled his eyes.

After I got booted out of the patrol car, I watched from the flagpole as they drove Granny away. I was sorry they left off the siren and the lights. I knew that inside that car Granny was sorry, too.

Just the day before, my brother Patrick had tried to talk me out of riding to school with Granny. He'd found me on the carport, throwing clumps of dirt at the chain-link fence that separated our yard from the gas station next door. The owner's cat was staring at me from out beside the free air pump, but I ignored it. I don't like cats as a rule.

"Tomorrow's your first day of seventh grade," Patrick said, pulling up an overturned paint bucket and taking a seat. I nodded. It was a dumb thing for him to say. I could have said something dumb back, like, "Yeah, and tomorrow's your first day of ninth grade, big whoop," but I wasn't in the mood.

Patrick scooped up a handful of crumbled concrete and aimed it at the cat, which was now sniffing at the fence like it was thinking about coming over for a visit. "If I was you, I'd take the bus to school," he said. "Granny's been driving you since you were in second grade. You've got to figure that's long enough."

"Don't want to take the bus," I told him. "I tried it once, but the exhaust fumes turned me green."

Patrick shook his head. "Beats everybody seeing Granny drop you off at the front of the school. Seventh grade's different from sixth grade. People start to notice it when your crazy grandmother drives you around all over town.

You want them to think you're weird, too?"

I picked at a piece of rubber coming off of my tennis shoe. People already thought I was weird. Between Granny and my juvenile delinquent brothers and sister and the fact that I lived in an old brick shoe box on a two-lane highway instead of in some shiny new suburban home, I didn't have much hope of them thinking otherwise. "I don't care what them fart blowers think," I told Patrick. "Why's it matter so much to you?"

Patrick stood up and shoved his hands in his pockets. Just then the gas station cat wormed its way through a hole in the fence and made a beeline for the carport. Patrick kicked at it and missed. "I don't care if people like you or not."

"So why are you here talking to me?"

He didn't say anything for a minute, just looked left, then right, like he was in a spy movie and the enemy was nearby. Finally he cleared his throat and said, "Daddy said he'd buy me a Big Mac and Super Size fries if I told you not to take rides from Granny anymore."

I snorted. "Daddy don't care who gives me a

ride to school. He's just looking to make Granny mad."

Patrick grinned. "Man, them two will give each other hell till one of them keels over dead."

My dad and Granny had been feuding for as long as I could remember. The only thing they ever had in common was my mom, and once she was gone, they didn't even have that. My sister, Summer, said they were both so mad about my mom dying they'd spend the rest of their lives taking it out on each other.

The gas station cat snaked its way around my ankles like it thought now maybe we could be friends. I scratched its ears without really meaning to. I didn't want to be friends with that cat or anybody else I could think of. Didn't want to go to school the next day either, especially since it was still August and way too hot for thinking.

Mostly I just wanted to ride around in Granny's truck and think about going camping out in the woods. I'd been camping two times in my life, and those trips were stuck on rerun in my brain. Whenever my mind needed somewhere to go, I pushed the camping-trip button on the inside of my head, and all the sudden I was putting river rocks in a circle to make a campfire. Made my whole body get peaceful remembering it.

After I'd watched the police car head out to the main road, I made my way down the hall to my first-period English class, going as slow as I could. I knew it would be a letdown after Granny's arrest, and I was right about that, son. Soon as I pushed open the door, a whole room of snot-nosed kids started giggling and twittering like flea-bitten parrots. Somebody called out, "Nice parking job!"

I ignored their sorry butts. The teacher motioned me over to a desk front and center and then checked her clipboard.

"Are you Tobin?" she asked. "Tobin McCauley?"

She pronounced it wrong, though, more like McCully. "That ain't how you say it," I told her, taking my seat. "It's McCauley that rhymes with holly."

"Ain't!" a low voice croaked like a bullfrog

from the back of the room, and then there was a chorus of bullfrogs calling "ain't, ain't, ain't," with a smart-aleck cricket chirping "redneck, redneck" behind it. A whole different voice, a boy's, only it was pitched high and singsongy, called out, "*Ain't* ain't a word!"

The teacher ignored the frogs and the cricket, but the last comment got her attention. "What makes you think it's not a word?" she asked. She walked to her desk, picked up a dictionary, and headed to the back row, where she handed it to a jughead named Cody Peters. "Look it up and tell me if it's in there."

Cody took the book from her. He didn't look too happy about having his little joke turned into an assignment. "I'll do what I can, ma'am," he said, this time in a slow, countrified voice. "*Ain't* starts with *a*, right?"

That got a good laugh from the spitwads around the room. "Stop talking and start looking," the teacher told him. She leaned against the desk in front of him, her arms folded across her chest. Cody ruffled through a few pages, then ran his finger down a row of words. After a few seconds he looked up at the teacher, his face all full of mock wonder. "Gosh, gee, ma'am, it sure enough is right here."

The teacher took the book from him and snapped it shut. "So maybe *ain't* is a word after all," she said, sounding victorious. She turned as she passed by me and gave me a big wink, like the victory was mine, too.

I put my head on my desk. That's all I needed, a teacher who wanted to be my hero. I closed my eyes and pictured a river. I was walking across it in knee-high rubber boots, carrying a mess of fish in a net. I could see a tent on the other side, smoke rising from the campfire.

I fell asleep before I made it over. Next thing I knew, there was a crow cawing in my ear, only it turned out to be the bell ringing for second period. I stood up slow, yawning my way back into the seventh grade and out to the hallway, where the rest of my useless day was waiting for me.

Looking for another great book?
Find it
IN THE MIDDLE.

Fun, fantastic books for kids
in the in-be**TWEEN** age.

IntheMiddleBooks.com

IRRESISTIBLE FICTION
from Edgar Award–winning author
FRANCES O'ROARK DOWELL!

TROUBLE
THE WATER

THE SECRET
LANGUAGE
OF GIRLS

THE KIND OF
FRIENDS
WE USED TO BE

THE SOUND OF
YOUR VOICE...
ONLY REALLY
FAR AWAY

ANYBODY
SHINING

DOVEY COE

WHERE I'D
LIKE TO BE

CHICKEN BOY

THE SECOND
LIFE OF
ABIGAIL WALKER

SHOOTING
THE MOON

FALLING IN

atheneum

SUMMER'S YEAR HAS BEEN FILLED WITH LOTS OF THINGS, but luck sure hasn't been one of them. So it's no surprise when things go from bad to worse. But if she can't find a way to swing her family's fortune around, they could lose everything—from their jobs as migrant workers to the very house they live in. Desperate to help, Summer takes action. After all, there's just no way things can get any *worse* . . . right?

By CYNTHIA KADOHATA, the Newbery Medal-winning author of KIRA-KIRA

PRINT AND EBOOK EDITIONS AVAILABLE

Caitlyn Dlouhy Books
atheneum simonandschuster.com/kids